BEST
LESBIAN EROTICA
OF THE YEAR

VOLUME THREE

BEST
LESBIAN EROTICA
OF THE YEAR

VOLUME THREE

Edited by

SACCHI GREEN

CLEiS
PRESS

Published in the United States by Cleis Press, an imprint of Start Midnight, LLC, 101 Hudson Street, Thirty-Seventh Floor, Suite 3705, Jersey City, NJ 07302.

Printed in the United States.
Cover design: Scott Idleman/Blink
Cover photograph: iStock
Text design: Frank Wiedemann

First Edition.
10 9 8 7 6 5 4 3 2 1

Trade paper ISBN: 978-1-62778-286-9
E-book ISBN: 978-1-62778-500-6

CONTENTS

INTRODUCTION

We open a book hoping to be taken somewhere—to faraway places, into the lives and inner thoughts of intriguing characters, or into times past or even unexplored depths of ourselves. If the book is classed as erotica, we also expect to be intensely stirred both sensually and emotionally. The beauty of an anthology is that we can expect to be taken in multiple directions, and meet an assortment of characters with a wide range of viewpoints. The drawback is that with short stories we often wish for more time with these characters, these sensations, these adventures. But writers with a special gift for short fiction can still draw us deeply into the brief length of their work, with multidimensional characters, vivid settings, intriguing story arcs, and, of course, sex as intrinsic to the story as any setting.

I've been lucky enough in two previous volumes of this series to be the editor who gets to read the flood of submissions and decide which of the best, in my opinion, should be included. I could never fit all of the very best into the limited space of a single anthology, so I try for a balance, and as wide a variety of themes and styles as possible, especially those I haven't seen before. Originality is high on my wish list.

Here are some hints as to where the stories I chose will take you, and what you may find there. Could there be a better start than the fantasy-fulfillment story, "Ninjutsu," set on a plane high above the Pacific en route from Tokyo to Honolulu? And what could feel more real than longtime lovers waking in the "Morning Fog" of San Francisco? How about touring the South of France in "Perfume," a massage in a Moroccan public bath in "Fuck Me Like a Canadian," a cabin "Where There's Smoke" in the snowy North Country, and the surveillance area above the ceiling of a Las Vegas casino where "Oliver: Twisted" begins?

New York City figures in at least three stories, playing different roles. In "The Auction," the city is an artsy background for socialite fundraisers. In "Trying Submission," it's an upscale background for a decidedly non-upscale character. And the Harlem of 1931 in "Sweet of My Heart" is the home of a Peace Mission's free meals where even a dance hall girl could be fed.

While most of the stories have contemporary settings, two more are set, at least partially, in the past. If you're old enough to have been swept up in the rock and blues bands frenzy of the '60s and '70s, you may catch the significance of September 1970, and even if you aren't that old, you'll find out in "Jani-Lyn's Dragon." And in "Still Marching," old friends who met and parted twenty-five years ago at a march for abortion rights in Washington, DC, bump into each other at a present-day march in Philadelphia.

There are various themes included in the anthology. I had quite a few submissions featuring coffeehouse encounters, but "Husher" is the one I chose for its deft and evocative style. There were also several submissions involving cancer, something I hadn't seen before, and others referring to trauma from past abuse; I went with "Fearless," which included both, along with a beautifully uplifting conclusion. Of the several stories I received featuring differently abled or neuro-atypical characters, I settled on "Trying Submission," with a vulnerable character who lingers vividly in my mind. On another tack, "The Night Shift" proves to be just the right time for accidental phone sex. Then the familiar professor/former student theme of "Rules" travels in unexpected directions and gets as steamily entertaining as they come, while the queer bookstore in "Rainbow's End" provides an ideal place for a hesitant would-be writer to find just what she hardly dared hope for. And in the beautifully balanced "Yin and Yang," a contemporary ballet dancer and her lighting-technician lover make the perfect team, while the writing, alternating between lyrical and straightforward, makes the perfect presentation of their story.

Yes, all of these stories include hot, intense sex, in its many-splendored manifestations. I'll leave you to discover those, scene by scene. A word of caution: you may not get jet lag from this journey, but a suitable recovery period between stories is highly recommended. Trust me.

Sacchi Green
Amherst, MA

NINJUTSU

Valerie Alexander

Rain is falling onto the tarmac. It's a soft rain, small puddles reflecting the red and blue airport lights. From the gate window I watch the drizzle, as if concerned that my flight out of Tokyo will be grounded. But really I'm standing at the window to assess my fellow passengers behind me, all reflected in the glass. And to show off my dark-red wrap dress and spiked black heels, which have drawn some curious looks. Most everyone at the gate is dressed for comfort, the better to sleep through the red-eye flight to Honolulu.

We're flying on a 747 tonight. From the number of people behind me, it doesn't seem the flight is full. That'll make things easier.

I adjust the enormous tote bag cutting into my shoulder and look down the tarmac as far as I can. Baggage handlers are driving their carts through the rain. For a moment I envy them—what a life that would be, working around planes at night instead of in office cubicles in the daytime. Then again, maybe planes wouldn't be as sexually fascinating if they were my job.

Our 747 lands. Everyone looks out the window. The dress is planned, but this gesture isn't: I put my hands on my hips and lift them, raising the dress slightly. Just a few inches, from my knees to almost midway up my thighs. Still gazing out at the rain, like it was an unconscious gesture, like I'm lost in thought. Then I release the dress to search through my bag, frowning with preoccupation, and turn.

More than a few people are watching me. Some men think they saw the accidental leg show of a respectable woman. But other women aren't fooled, I can tell by their wry, calculating eyes. I find a seat and play with my phone, bringing my long black hair over my shoulder and setting my bag next to my heels. I'm stealthy as I scan potential targets. The American college girl in the sweatshirt is too young—I need someone older, with self-control. A thirtyish blonde gives me a gorgeous smile but she seems to be playing trophy wife to the older executive next to her. Maybe the jock would do, the one who's all tanned muscles and unlaced tennis shoes. She looks like a few conquests have passed through her hands. And then there's the butch woman with short black hair and a handsome, tired face. She's wearing a classic white T-shirt and jeans, arms spread insolently to claim the seats on either side of her.

Then we're boarding. As always the procedure of finding my window seat, stuffing my carry-on in the overhead compartment, and locking my seat belt gives me an excited flutter of trepidation. I lean my head back against the seat and close my eyes almost all the way, until I look asleep. This way I can still keep a watch on the passengers and make note of their seats—but unfortunately I am too far up to see much.

The flight attendant delivers her routine. Emergency exits, which restrooms we can wait in line for and which we can't. The price of Wi-Fi, movie headsets, and drinks. I tune her out and watch the rain streak the window. A baggage vehicle is still parked beneath our plane, the handlers efficient as they throw suitcases into the 747's lower deck.

I amend my earlier fantasy. I wouldn't have a job on the tarmac at night but a stealth vocation. I'd wait in the shadows of the plane's giant wheels and then, when the baggage handler drove up her cart, I'd walk out of the darkness toward her without a word. I would be like a haunt, a succubus, who materialized under resting planes to unbutton the uniforms of hardworking women and lure them into the shadows. Sinking to my knees on the tarmac or maybe bending over with my dress up around my waist and my hands on the tires as they fucked me from behind. Then vanishing without a word.

I don't know where these types of thoughts come from.

Tokyo's neon glow falls away like an abandoned electric birthday cake as we rise into the sky. Eight hours until we touch down in the soft Honolulu dawn. My seat companion wants to know if I'm from Japan or the States and if I'm traveling for business or pleasure; she's not being nosy, just making what she considers polite conversation. I don't mention that this is not a vacation for me but an exodus. That I'm leaving Tokyo, and the woman I lived with there, forever. My seatmate would think a divorce is something I'd need to be consoled about and just possibly she might probe for some kind of lesbian details to titillate her book club with back home. So I just say I'm looking forward to the Honolulu beaches, smile, and put my headphones on—a social code internationally understood.

She reads for about an hour before turning off the light and going to sleep. Many of the passengers seem to be asleep, though it's not terribly late by Tokyo time. A few reading lights still shine down from the cabin ceiling, other rows illuminated by the glow of laptops and tablets. I turn on my side and stare out the window. The clouds have a tinge of pink against the indigo night. If I ever won the lottery, I would fly internationally every weekend. I would never leave airports; I would be untraceable, a ninja of the air. And it would all be for moments like this, the darkness of the cabin and the thrum of the engines disguising me as I carefully slide my hand up my thigh. Going slow, like a stranger would, testing the waters of my receptivity.

Which a real stranger did a few years ago. It was shortly after I moved to Japan, on a different red-eye flight. She was straight, I thought, a businesswoman in a well-cut suit who didn't speak to me before takeoff. Her hand dangled from the armrest at first, then gradually draped over it until her fingers grazed my thigh. She seemed asleep. I didn't move her hand. It was a cheap thrill, a strange woman's fingertips on my leg, an inch from the hem of my dress. Was it really an accident? I couldn't tell. I opened my legs experimentally and she shifted, eyes closed, fingers moving up my leg. I opened my legs a bit wider and her hand moved in deeper, fully between my thighs. It rested there for a full minute or so as my pussy throbbed wildly—and then as her thumb stroked my inner thigh, horror at what I was doing shot through me like a scalding rocket. I got up and went to the restroom, where I furiously rubbed myself off. When I got back to my seat, the woman seemed to be deep in a nap and didn't touch me.

Just an interlude. Something that could be framed so many ways—an opportunist, like the arrogant rugby player who used to play with my breasts in the dorm shower; a transnational sleepwalker; a mind reader.

But it didn't matter what the businesswoman was. It mattered what I was: an adulteress, opening my legs for a stranger five months after moving in with the woman I said was the love of my life. And when I went to my partner a few weeks later, guilty yet still racked with dreams of anonymous sex, she looked disdainful. "Why would you even want that?" she said when I asked her to play a game of pretend with me. My shame intensified. I should be content with our cuddly sex three or four times a week. But the fantasy came back stronger than the shame, and soon I was getting off to it on a regular basis, imagining myself with anonymous women I saw in public gardens and museums, stores. Which was as far as I let it go, until now.

My panties are soaked. I shift in my seat and carefully hook my finger through the elastic, then pull them down my legs. No one can see me, but I'm still careful as I slip them over my heels and stuff them in my bag. I curl under the blanket again, lifting one leg slightly. It's important to be quiet, though I don't think anyone could hear the movement of my fingers over the dull roar of the plane. And anyway, that's not what I want tonight. My fingers on my cunt feel wrong. Too familiar. Pointless. I close my eyes and remember the businesswoman stroking my inner thigh, my certainty then that she was about to take over my pussy with silent confidence and mastery—and for the eight thousandth time I wish I had let her continue.

Suddenly hot and restless, I sit up straight and shake off the blanket.

The airplane cabin is quiet. It's fairly late Tokyo time now and most of the passengers are asleep. Three rows ahead of me burns one overhead reading light.

I twist in my seat to survey the rows behind me. Darkness. Pure darkness.

I get up and climb carefully over my sleeping seatmate. The obvious choice is the front restroom just seven rows away. Instead I make way down the aisle to the back.

Muted, tiny lights embedded in the floor guide the way. I hold on to the seats as I pass through the dark cabin, taking my time.

My pussy feels so wet and full that I want to take my dress off right here and proceed naked through the dark. My eyes adjust well enough to the dark that I catch her watching me—the woman with the short dark hair, leaning her head back and evaluating me with a dark, calculating gaze.

And the seat next to her is empty.

I continue through the dark cabin. The two rear restrooms are occupied. I wait, noticing that in the very last row there's a suspicious movement under a blanket—it's the college girl and she's none too subtle in what she's doing under her blanket. Apparently I'm not the only one who gets inspired on night flights.

Someone else lumbers down the aisle toward me. A thick-necked, fiftyish man. "Both full?" he murmurs to me in apparent courtesy of the sleeping passengers around us. I nod and then one of the restroom doors open—and I vanish into the restroom and lock myself inside.

I'm so wet that my thighs are sticking together. I run my fingers over my pussy and smear them on my neck, between my tits. Then I pee and wash up, fix a bit of smeared mascara, and leave.

No one's waiting. Good. The college girl seems to have joined the other passengers in slumberland. There's not a single reading light in this section of the cabin. Slowly I make my way up the aisle until I locate the row of the dark-haired woman I exchanged gazes with earlier. The seat next to her is still empty.

I slip into it without looking at her.

"Could I have a blanket please?" I ask a passing flight attendant. If she remembers this seat was empty before, she doesn't blink. Instead she brings me a navy airline blanket and I thank her and fluff it out. Still without looking at my new seatmate, I lift the armrest between her seat and mine. Then I curl up under the blanket, facing away from her, and settle in.

Nothing happens. Maybe she thinks I've ordered too many

drinks, a woman lost in the wrong row of seats. Maybe she's got a wife at home. Or maybe she's just not into anonymous sex with aggressive femmes.

I shift a bit under the blanket, gradually moving my ass back until it's close to her hip. If she ignores me, I'll leave.

She shifts, just a restless passenger trying to get comfortable on a red-eye flight. But now our bodies are touching.

Under the blanket, I undo the wrap dress and pull it up to my hips. Then I gather the blanket tighter around my front, drawing it up until I can feel the cool cabin air teasing my bare ass.

More movement from my butch stranger. It starts with her knuckles resting against the back of my thigh. I bring my legs up closer to my front, uncertain of what exactly is exposed back there but knowing it's a lot. And something lightly brushes my ass—fingertips, then an entire calloused palm on my left cheek. My heart is pounding. I think I might come as soon as she touches me for real.

But she takes her time, feeling my ass, squeezing it, not concerned at all with trying to feign a sleepy accident like my previous airplane stranger. This is a woman who understands why I came to her in the dark plane. Her fingers dip between my legs and push right inside me, two of them, filling my cunt so insistently that I bury my head and bite my arm. Oh god, this is going so much farther than I really thought it would. I'm going so much farther than I thought I would. Waves of heat and excitement soak me, starting at my scalp and sweeping down my body, stiffening my nipples and filling my clit with a tight electric tension.

I might need more than this, getting fingered so thoroughly on a plane by a silent handsome woman. I might need a lot more. I roll back toward her, just lying back in my seat now, and spread my legs under the blanket. She goes back in from the front. But this time she doesn't finger me; instead she plays with my entire pussy, lightly pinching my lips and tugging them a little, circling my clit. I keep my eyes closed. I've forgotten exactly what her face looked like in the airport, and I like not knowing.

Then she tugs me across her lap. Oh no. I wasn't counting on this. I'm still on my back, across her legs, and I guess the flight attendants could take me for her wife, sleeping on her, if they walk by. But she doesn't seem to care about the flight attendants. She's feeling every part of me she can, running her hands over my breasts, down my stomach. Impatiently she pushes my dress all the way apart so I'm essentially naked under the blanket. Oh god. I remember how easily I could tell the college girl was touching herself under her blanket, and I realize anyone who walks up or down the aisle past us will notice there are two women moving suspiciously under the blanket, one with her legs spread.

But I can't stop. Her fingers are thrusting inside me again, and I'm riding them shamelessly, my breasts bouncing as she pulls the blanket down to expose them. Some tiny practical part of my brain wonders if we'll be arrested if caught, but it's all so exciting that I spread my legs wider.

And then she stops.

I squirm in complaint. She laughs a deep, low laugh and pulls the blanket back up to cover me again, then turns me on my side so I'm facing her crotch. I understand.

I take down her jeans as best I can. Her body is smooth and thick, with hard thigh muscles that give way to the surprise of her pussy—which is just a shadowy delta in the dark, but the heat and the smell of her fill my nostrils and take me to the heaven I've been dreaming of. Her lips spread out under my tongue like butterfly wings, gleaming and wet. Dipping my fingers inside her, I lick her swollen pink clit as best I can, not as deft as I'd normally be, but good enough that her thighs open farther, straining against her jeans. The soft squishy noises of my fingers moving in and out of her cunt tell me how much she wanted her own nameless fuck. My tongue swims over every creamy inch of her, licking up the honey from her inflamed slit. One muffled grunt and her hands clutch me as she comes, her hips rocking into my face so hard that I'm convinced she's going to wake someone up.

Then she pulls me up and positions me so I'm sitting on her lap. She can't possibly think we'll get away with this. But she's pushing inside me, going up my cunt until she's all the way in.

It feels so good I want to scream. She's holding me tightly, a good thing as I've lost almost total control. I pitch forward against her muscled arms, struggling to stay silent while she fucks me in a ragged, seesaw rhythm. Back and forth, back and forth. I'm hot, sweating, my hair hanging in my face. And then I look up and see that we have been caught—the blonde trophy wife across the aisle is shamelessly leaning over to watch while her husband sleeps next to her. So I pull down the blanket and give her a show, letting her see how two women can fuck each other blind. My stranger is losing control herself, not holding me quite as carefully now, and instead we're twisted in a kind of sideways doggie-style, she ramming me so forcefully that I drop my head and bite my arm as I explode in silence, squirting all over her lap and the seat until it's dripping down my thighs.

She lets go of me and sinks back into her seat, squeezing my tits in what seems to be a final thank-you and good-bye. I grope for my dress and wrap it around me as best as I can. The blonde smirks at me as I get up, legs shaking in my spiked heels. Continuing up the aisle again, this time I really have to grip the seat backs for balance as the tiny floor lights swim at me. At last I come to my row and climb over the woman next to me, jostling her a bit as I sink into my seat.

The view from my window is pure stars. We're nowhere right now. I love this moment between nations, between identities, between consequences. I revel in it for a moment, then pull my real clothes out of my bag and do another under-the-blanket performance—slipping into sweatpants and T-shirt, stuffing my dress in my tote. Then I pin up my long hair and pull on a sleep mask for a nap. Just a few hours now until I'm somewhere new, until I'm someone new. A woman of stealth and mastery, who can materialize in the arms of strangers and vanish before being captured.

MORNING FOG

Scout Rhodes

It's dark, still. I hear no predawn bird cacophony like I would at home, but there's a subtle uptick in cars passing on the city street below as morning commutes begin. I wake up early, always, having been born and bred on a farm, but this morning I wake up earlier, alert the moment I feel her shifting as she begins the slow swim upward from the depths of heavy sleep. Everything smells so different; her skin, the scent of her cat in the apartment, old books on the shelves, sandalwood soap, the West Coast fog that blankets the city overnight, this ancient wooden building hammered together just after the quake and fire, woolen carpets on the floor, remnants of last night's supper in unwashed pots in the sink.

I love it here. I carefully snake my arm around her waist as her hips move a little, big spoon and little spoon, and rest my hand on her warm, silky belly. I am wide awake, and waiting patiently. She is so soft, even as I brush the skin of her broad, naked shoulders with my lips, that I am compelled to gently stroke her belly hair as I would a kitten curled against me. I should let her sleep, but she's already waking on her own, and I desire her intensely.

Here we are, she and I, two old queers who have endured long, curious, circuitous lives that have brought us to this place, this morning, this moment. We're neither of us gold star *anything*, having fucked men, women, trans folk, and many, many people between the two of us. We've both borne, breastfed, and raised children created the "old-fashioned way," which makes us pariahs in certain hard-line lesbian circles. We both identified as bisexual in our youth, we've both married men in our time, we've both been subjected to degradation and abuse at masculine hands, but now we're both butch dykes, and we're both survivors. That's it— we're gold star *survivors*. Isn't that enough? It sure feels like a lot, after far more than a century of combined years.

Two gold star survivors who found each other in this crazy, neo-fascist cesspool that America has become, and we hold on to each other for dear life while living in the crosshairs. We hail from opposite coasts but managed to find each other, and we're not letting go. At this moment, we cling to each other in her bed in the heart of San Francisco. She is rousing from sleep, enfolded in my arms, her naked ass pressed against my belly, so inviting. I kiss her shoulders again and then the back of her closely shorn head, she wiggles and moans, and this is how it begins.

I trail my fingers softly up and down her belly, along the lines of her rib cage, brush against her right breast. Her nipple contracts and hardens into a perfect nub, which I roll between my fingertips like a red pebble plucked from the sand of Ocean Beach, like a memento. She whimpers as I stretch and pull her breast, arches her back, grinds her ass into my groin, and my own nipples contract in response, my clit jumps and thickens in its hood, a sudden surge of wet in my cunt oozes onto my thigh.

She is no longer sound asleep. The tattooed flock of birds on her torso are fluttering their wings, turning their heads this way and that, greeting the day.

I roll her onto her back, kiss the soft folds of skin on that long neck of hers. We are old people, both of us, and we are so hot for each other it drives us half mad. No one told me this would happen, this reawakening of desire after the half-century mark. It was like a surprise birthday party thrown by one's closest and dearest friends, unexpected and utterly delightful, warm and loving and with plentiful food and the best cake. My hand moves from her breast to languidly pry open her long legs. She is *toujours prêt*, always ready for me, slick with precome, clit swollen and protruding. How I long to take her engorgement into my mouth, to suck it like a candy, her flavor on my tongue like Turkish paste, sweet and salty and nutty.

I dip between her labia with my fingertips and stroke her cunt from clit to asshole, back and forth with a feather touch on this rare and wondrous canvas. Hips rise with each brushstroke, and I know she aches for my fingers, my fist inside her.

Like heartache, like a dream, I slip one finger inside her cunt, reaching to press the soft pad that fully wakes her lust. Her eyes flutter open and she looks at me, not yet able to speak, but I know exactly what she wants. I slide two fingers into her hole, three fingers, four, stretching her wide and deep. Now I'm on my knees between her pale, grasshopper legs, and I reach up with my left hand to tug and twist her right nipple, the favored one. Her body gently undulates, wavelike, with the combination of pain and pleasure.

I am so hungry for her, so very greedy. There is a trickle of precome, my own, sliding down my thigh and my clit throbs sympathetically, responding to her sensuous ripple. I turn my hand inside her, my thumb finds its way to that special spot to the side of her thickened clit, pressing into the flesh there until she shudders. Who am I to deny her the sensation she craves? I cup my thumb into my palm and push into her cunt slowly, turning and twisting, spiraling inward like a nautilus shell. Close my eyes and feel my way. She whispers, "Pl-pl-please," and with one more plunge and twist, my hand is inside her clutching cunt. My hand curls into a fist, thumb tucked inside, and I explore. My knuckles press against her cervix, I gauge her reaction and turn my fist again.

My left hand is on her right tit, kneading and pulling at the stretchy red nipple. My own emptiness torments me. I take her clit into my mouth, desperate to be filled, too, and suckle that tender organ. We are connected, the circuit is complete: hand, tit, mouth, clit, cunt, fist. I suck her wetly, slurping her clit as I would a raw oyster, salty with seawater. I am the anglerfish's mate, locked into her body; my purpose is to serve her pleasure. My fist belongs inside of her. I turn my hand again, twist her nipple, mouth her engorged cunt, and sense the growing come start in her belly, rolling forth like a full-moon tide.

I feel the planet spinning slowly as I turn and knuckle inside her slippery cunt. My fist is the axis around which everything whirls: clouds, continents, oceans, life. Fog drifts in through the open window and coats my skin, my hair, with moisture as if I were in the mossy forest back East. She is babbling now, meaningless fragments of words that tumble from her open mouth, urging me on. Her cunt begins a slow clenching pressure around my wrist as she squirms, flails, hands clutching at blankets, hips jerking, legs starting to shake. I breathe, "Come for me. I want you to come for me now." She roars skyward as she comes and it fills my ears, the sweetest music of sex and pleasure. Her cunt bruises my wrist in a circlet that I will feel for many days, remembering, as I lift my mug of tea, turn the doorknob, button a shirt, pick up my backpack.

One more turn of my fist inside her, one more twist of her nipple. My sharp teeth sink into her thigh, and she is coming again, ejaculating, gushing her come up my arm, yelling into the foggy room.

Our breaths are ragged as we ride out the aftershocks. I slowly unfurl my fist as I gently slide my hand from her cunt. I hold her to me as I mutter quiet and sweet endearments into her ears. I kiss her soft skin, her neck, her cheeks, her swollen lips. She drifts back into the dark waters of sleep; it is very early, after all. I pull the blankets up around her naked shoulders and tenderly tuck her in, and slide carefully out of the bed.

There is a robe on the chair, woolen and itchy but warm against the fog. I pull it on and glide barefoot across the apartment into the little kitchen to put on the kettle for tea, and dig around in the refrigerator for wild mushrooms, eggs, and goat cheese for our omelet breakfast. The cat appears from nowhere, like magic, and winds herself around my legs, begging for her morning kibble and fresh water. I pull back the curtain in the kitchen window to peer out at the fog as it rolls through the city streets. There is a hint of yellow and pink eastward over the building outlines, a few morning birds tentatively chirp, and the promise of another sweet day with my beloved is kept.

WHERE THERE'S SMOKE

M. Birds

"The woman in the woods been asking for you," Kyle said when June saw him, leaning over the pharmacist's counter.

"The hell she was."

"Well, not you specifically, but . . . you know. Your goods and services. Told her I'd pass the message on."

June chewed on her lower lip. "No thanks, man. What if she's a cop or something?"

Kyle snorted. He and June had grown up together, danced with each other at their high school's half-assed prom. June was still dreaming of leaving then—getting out of their tiny town, moving to the city, going to school. She'd had big, big plans.

"That woman ain't no cop." Kyle shook his head. "You've seen her."

June had seen her. Everyone in town had seen her walking through the slushy streets with boots that cost more than a month's rent. Some artsy type from the city, renting Frank Pinchbeck's cabin for the season. Even though the snow was finally melting, the woman in the woods seemed constantly wrapped in plaid and flannel, huge wool coats and cashmere scarves.

"Could have money," Kyle said, considering. "You should cut me in."

June rolled her eyes. But the next day, she filled her messenger bag and headed into the woods.

Her dad always told June she had a green thumb. Potted plants, even goddamn vases of flowers seemed to thrive when June touched them. The Wander-Inn wasn't exactly the place for a greenhouse, but June's dad kept the flower boxes full, built a raised garden plot round back where the parking stalls were. In summer there were always fresh pansies in the rooms, even when they were empty. June's dad was like that—a man with an eye for detail, and no sense of the big picture goddamn whatsoever.

When he died, and June and her mom realized how fucked the hotel was financially, they had a couple of choices. They could try to sell or they could beg, borrow, and steal from everyone they knew in the hopes of getting their heads even somewhat above water. June learned pretty quick (an eighteen-year-old with big plans) that her green thumb could be used for more than just planting pansies.

She went to the city and bought a *High Times* magazine on her nineteenth birthday. By the time she turned twenty, she had enough for lights and soil and seeds, and by twenty-one she was a business owner. She didn't grow a lot, but enough to keep the bills paid, enough to make sure her mom never had to worry about where their next meal would come from. And she didn't sell to kids, and it was all legal now anyway, right? June tried to justify it to herself on nights when she'd had a bit too much to drink.

She didn't end up going anywhere, not to the city and not to school. How could she leave her mom on a sinking ship like the Wander-Inn? No, June stayed and made money and worked the front desk, staying up late to read about fertilizer and pH levels. She didn't smoke the stuff herself (got all paranoid and red-faced that one time in high school) but she lived in a tourist town, and there were no end of willing customers.

June stayed. And if she dreamed some nights about smoke-filled city bars where women wore leather and dark lipstick, well—no one needed to know about that.

The woman in the woods was smaller up close. She answered the door in a sweater, peering out at June with wide, light eyes. June almost took a step back at the sight of her high cheekbones and long neck. The woman looked like a bird made of glass. June was afraid of breaking her.

"Kyle—from the pharmacy," she said awkwardly by way of introduction. "He told me you were looking for me."

The woman said nothing, just blinked at June with long eyelashes. It was impossible to tell how old she was—maybe late thirties? Older than June but not much. Her skin was flawless, blonde hair razored short against her skull. June felt shabby by comparison, dressed like a hillbilly in her oversized jeans and her dad's old shearling coat.

"I'm June." She stuck out her hand, because fuck knew what else she was going to do.

"Miriam." The woman in the woods didn't shake June's hand and June noticed the curves of her long fingers, the way they stuck tight together like she was wearing mittens, knuckles round and swollen. "What do you want exactly?"

"I wanted to see . . . " June paused, chewing her lip. "If there was anything you needed. Kyle said there might be."

"Kyle from the pharmacy." Miriam crossed her arms. She

glanced back into her cabin, and then out toward the path leading through the woods. "Did you walk here?"

"Yeah. Didn't take long. I live in the Wander-Inn. I mean, I own it. Or my family does."

"Is that the one that looks like an Alpine resort? It's very . . . very, um . . . "

June laughed and nodded. "Like a time warp, isn't it? Like someone from the sixties saw one postcard of Switzerland and then dropped acid and thought 'I should build that.'"

"I was going to say—quaint."

"Sure you were."

Miriam's mouth curved just slightly, the smile there and gone so fast that June almost missed it.

"I suppose you should come in." Miriam stood aside, gesturing with one thin arm through the doorway.

June slid out of her wet boots, hung her coat on the hook by the doorway. She didn't even try to pretend she wasn't looking around. She'd never been inside Frank's cabin, had no idea he'd spruced it up so nice for tourists. It had high ceilings and shiny hardwood floors. A fire was going in the grate in front of a vintage-looking leather couch, artfully draped with a bright wool blanket, and most of the flat surfaces had jarred beeswax candles flickering. June whistled low—then immediately blushed. Christ, this woman probably thought she was some bumpkin who'd never seen fire before.

"It's nice," she said to cover her embarrassment.

"It suits my purposes." Miriam followed her in, looking uncertain. "Do you want—tea or water or anything?"

"I'm good." June sat down on the couch, laying her messenger bag across her lap. "So what is it? Arthritis? Just your hands or . . . "

Miriam crossed the room to the small attached kitchen, busying herself with a kettle that needed filling. She looked a bit furtive, like someone used to hiding things.

"Rheumatoid in my hands, chronic pain everywhere else," she answered, not looking at June. "Gets worse when I'm under stress. The end of my marriage didn't help."

"I'm sorry." June felt suddenly out of her depth. "Is that why you're here then? Getting away from it all?"

"I suppose so." Miriam set the kettle boiling, taking two large pottery mugs out of the cupboard. It looked like June was getting tea whether she needed it or not. "Trying to do some work as well. I teach English at VIU."

Of course she does, June thought. This polished, articulate woman screamed "English professor" from the tips of her blonde hair to the toes of her expensive boots.

"The thought of staying in my house, the house where we—it was simply untenable. I had to go somewhere." Miriam pulled at the sleeves of her sweater. June watched the movements of her hands, nails short but manicured. "So how do we do this?"

Oh, right—business. June had almost forgotten. "Well. I can tell you a little bit about what I've got. Or you can tell me what you're looking for. Have you done this before?"

"In college." Miriam laughed shyly. It changed her whole face, that laugh. June hadn't even realized she was pretty until that moment, and now she felt like someone had punched her in the heart. "A long time ago, as you may have guessed. And last year, when the pain was really bad, I used an oil. I had a prescription." She lifted her eyes defensively, as if June was in any place to judge.

"Did it help?"

"Not really. It made me tired."

"Okay. What I'm thinking for you . . . " June unzipped her bag and pulled out a mason jar full of dried green buds. "Widow's Walk."

Miriam came closer, sitting down in the armchair across from June. There was a crease between her light eyebrows.

"Rather grim name."

"I've got another client with chronic pain, he swears by this stuff. Good for inflammation, doesn't make you sleepy, no paranoia. So I've heard anyway."

"You don't—"

"Not my thing. Not to say I wouldn't smoke it if I needed to, just—not recreationally."

Miriam studied her, and June wondered what she saw. A solidly built thirty-year-old, with curly brown hair and a cardigan she bought secondhand. A criminal, showing up at a stranger's house and trying to sell her drugs. A nobody in snow-damp jeans.

"Can I be honest?" Miriam asked suddenly. "You don't look like a drug dealer. If I imagined one, they wouldn't look like you."

"Do I need an eye patch, or a scar or something?"

Again, Miriam laughed and June was punched in the solar plexus. That laugh took the air right out of her lungs.

"That would be a start. How much?"

"Thirty dollars for an eighth. That'll last you awhile. And I can always hook you up with more if you need it. Maybe with the quiet and the fresh air, you'll be feeling better."

"Maybe."

"Do you want to try it?" June had taken one of the smaller buds out of the jar, and was fishing out her grinder. "I'm assuming you don't have a pipe or anything, but I could roll you something. No point buying a bunch if it makes you sick."

Miriam smiled, wryly. "First one's free, is that it?"

There was something indulgent about the way her mouth formed words, even though it was a tiny, razor-sharp sort of mouth. Miriam dragged her teeth against her lips when she spoke, like each sentence was being forced out of her.

"If you like," June answered, remembering that she had been asked a question.

The kettle dinged sharply.

Miriam got up, going into the kitchen and bringing back two mugs of steaming tea. When she handed one to June, the pottery was scalding against her fingertips.

Instead of returning to the armchair, Miriam sat down beside her on the couch. Now June could smell the sweet bitterness of their tea, and the odd musty scent of Miriam's sweater. There was something else, too—perfume or shampoo that smelled like some sort of flower. Orchids. June breathed through her mouth and tasted it on her tongue.

Yeah, orchids.

"Will you show me?" Miriam asked, setting her tea down on the coffee table. "How you . . . I don't think I can."

June didn't know what she was talking about until Miriam lifted her hands, gesturing to the grinder and rolling papers June had brought out of her bag.

"Oh. Sure," June said, feigning a casualness she did not feel. She was acutely aware of the clumsiness of her hands as she folded up a filter, ground the plant fine as ashes. When she had packed the joint full enough, she brought the paper to her lips, licking along the seam to seal it. The only sound she could hear was the snap of the fire and Miriam's steady breathing.

"There you are," she said, offering the joint to Miriam. "Easy peasy."

Miriam spun it between her fingers as if unsure what to do with it. She looked like an old movie star smoking her first cigarette.

"Do you have a light?"

"Um." June had not been expecting that, and was still mentally shrieking at herself for the "easy peasy" bit, Christ, what was she, four? "You don't have to smoke it now. I mean, you can, but . . . "

"I'd like to. If that's all right. In case—well, I'm a bit nervous."

June should have found that funny, but she didn't. Instead, she reached into her bag for her zippo lighter, feeling a bit apprehensive. She didn't usually stay with clients while they smoked, she didn't usually drink goddamn tea with them. She was usually in and gone, with money in her pocket enough to get the electrician off her back.

"Here." June clicked the lighter and held out the flame. Miriam leaned in, joint held against her lips. As the tip turned black, she sucked lightly in and tilted her head back. June watched her pulse beat in her throat, watched a soft exhale of smoke roll out of Miriam's mouth like perfume.

"All right?" June asked.

Miriam nodded.

"My wife rolled her own cigarettes," she said on the next exhale, closing her eyes. "Fuck, I mean my ex-wife. Still getting used to that."

Fuck, she had said, a jarring discord between that word and her elegant mouth. It took a moment for the rest of the sentence to catch up with June.

Miriam had had a wife. Miriam was gay—or a lesbian, or bi or whatever. None of which mattered, it didn't matter who she slept with or wanted to sleep with. She was June's client. They didn't know each other. Not at all.

"What happened?" June asked, even though she knew she shouldn't. Maybe it was the smoke in the air or the goddamn beeswax candles but her mouth was asking questions it had no business to. "With you and your wife?"

Miriam studied the glowing ember of the joint. "Are you married?" she asked instead of answering.

"No."

"But you're . . . " Miriam gestured gracefully with one hand. "You know. Involved with someone."

"Uh, no."

"Oh." Miriam traced her lips with the tip of her ring finger, a movement that June couldn't help but follow. It was a distracted movement, and Miriam's eyes were far away, but even so it seemed dangerously intimate. "How old are you?"

"Why?" June blurted, skin prickling.

"I hate not being able to place someone. Should I guess?"

"Jesus, no. I don't want to hear it. I'm thirty-two."

"Hmm." Miriam took a slow, deep drag and waited a moment before slowly breathing out. "I think that's enough of that for now." She crossed the room to stub the joint out in an unlit candle, leaving it there smoldering. When she returned to the couch, she sat a little closer, her shoulder nearly leaning against June's.

"She didn't love me anymore. My wife. That's what happened." Miriam ran her hands over the short, blonde hairs on her head. "How many people have you kissed?"

Three. June had kissed three people in her entire life.

Kyle from the pharmacy was her first, both of them completely drunk at a pit party in grade ten. Grade ten was a bit old for a first kiss according to all of June's friends, but it didn't feel significant at the time. It felt like something to get out of the way. Felt like kicking in a door or jump-starting an engine. Violent and necessary.

Kyle puked shortly after and June puked the next morning, so the whole scene left a grimy taste in her mouth. She didn't kiss Kyle again.

Her second kiss was better: Dylan Samson, on a class trip to the city. He was just on the outskirts of cool, his features delicate and pretty as a girl's, and he'd barely spoken to June before that trip. On the last night, Dylan's friend snuck a mickey of vodka into their hotel, and they hung out in his room after the chaperones were asleep, passing it back and forth among a group of them. June had just turned eighteen, and Dylan's pink lips tasted like cinnamon when she kissed him. All his friends hooted and jeered but by then June was too tipsy to give a damn. She and Dylan made out in the en suite bathroom with the door locked, and fooled around for a bit after the trip was over. It clearly didn't mean anything to either of them. Dylan hung around town for a few years after graduation, but by that time he and June were more friends than anything else, and he left for some job on the pipelines not long after.

Her third kiss was the worst.

There was—a girl. Woman. June had been twenty-six. The woman had only been in town for eight months, teaching at the local school while Alison Meadows was off having her baby. June had seen the woman around town but hadn't really spoken to her until one night at the Stag. It was crowded for once (all the snowboarders in town) and they ended up sharing a table. It had been karaoke night and the woman had sung "Edge of Seventeen" with a pint glass in her hand, while June fell wildly and stupidly in love with her. They kissed for the first time five days later. June had always really considered herself bisexual in the dark, secret privacy of her mind, but that first kiss with the woman felt nothing like her previous two. They spent the night together, and June walked home the next morning feeling like a sun that was rising.

They slept together most nights after that, June (still deeply in the closet) sneaking the woman in and out of her room at the Wander-Inn, the two of them shaking with silent laughter that turned into gasps when their bodies touched. They were together right up until the woman's contract ended, and she had to leave.

The woman told June it'd "been fun."

June didn't kiss anyone else after that.

* * *

"Three," June answered before she could ask herself why she was answering. Before she could tell herself it was none of this stranger's business. "Just—three."

"Three," Miriam repeated, tilting her head. Again, June was reminded of a bird, fine-boned and soft-feathered.

"Going through a bit of a dry spell." June shrugged. "It happens."

"No one at the Wander-Inn to catch your eye?"

"Ha, no. When we even get customers it's like—happy families or frat-boy snowboarders."

"Too cool for the frat boys?"

June paused. She took a breath.

"Not too cool." Just say it, fucking say it. "Too—uh—gay." There. There. The sky hadn't fallen, the cabin hadn't caught fire. June was fine. It was fine. "So."

Miriam said nothing. She folded her hands and then unfolded them.

"They don't hurt so much," she said at last, looking down at her hands. "Should it happen this fast? Or is it just a placebo effect? Or does that even matter if it's working?" She laughed softly. Was it June's imagination or was Miriam even closer to her? It seemed like the woman was shifting with each breath, leaning in until June could feel Miriam's breath against her face.

"Should I roll you some more?"

"Yes." Miriam looked up, pinning June in a clear, pale gaze. For a moment, June couldn't move, couldn't even swallow or breathe. "But first—"

"But first?" June's heart was hammering in her chest, a feeling like adrenaline or panic.

"But—if you wanted . . . "

"If I wanted . . . "

June stopped speaking at the first touch of Miriam's hand. The tips of her fingers were rough and warm as they traced June's knuckles, slipped into the sleeve of her cardigan to stroke her wrist. June could feel Miriam's thumb drawing a circle against her thundering pulse point.

"If you wanted," Miriam said, lifting her other hand to tangle in June's hair. June's hair was perpetually wild and knotted with curls, but it seemed to part like water beneath Miriam's fingers. June wanted to purr like a cat until Miriam's hand suddenly tightened, tugging her roughly closer.

June's fourth kiss was the best one.

Miriam's mouth was warm from tea and tasted like smoke. Her tongue was insistent, sliding between June's lips without hesitation, tasting the back of her throat and sucking the breath from her lungs. It was a hostage-taking kiss, and June would gladly have put her hands up in surrender if those hands weren't latching on to Miriam's sweater, pulling their bodies together.

A voice in June's head was screaming at her, saying things like "married" and "rebound," but June tried to ignore it in favor of biting down on Miriam's lower lip.

"Come here," Miriam said with a gasp, leaning back against the couch and pulling June up onto her lap. June felt huge on top of her, a great beast compared to the elegant woman between her legs. She tried to ignore that thought as well.

"Take this off." Miriam tugged at June's cardigan, pulling at the neck of it so that she could lean up and fasten her teeth there. "I want to see you. Please, can you?"

"Yes." June kissed the word into her mouth and then promptly forgot what she was answering. Miriam's tongue licked sweetly against June's own, and June tilted her head, opened up to more of it. She felt Miriam's hands at the small of her back, pulling her closer against her. The voice in June's head shouted "stoned on drugs that you sold her," and that—that was something June really couldn't ignore.

"Wait." She pulled back from Miriam's kiss. "Wait."

Miriam watched her, breathing silent but rapid. Her hands still moved restlessly up and down June's back, as if she couldn't help herself.

"You're high and I'm not."

"So?"

"I don't want you to do anything you change your mind about later."

Miriam rolled her eyes. "Darling—first of all, I barely smoked anything and I'm well in control of my faculties. And second, I really, really want to touch you, and my hands don't hurt for the first time in months, and as the clear-headed one of course you are welcome to say no, but please don't say no because you think you're—taking advantage. My god, if anything the opposite is true."

"You're taking advantage of me?"

Miriam raised one eyebrow, the corner of her mouth curling to match. "The older woman . . . luring a young innocent up to her secluded cabin in the woods . . . "

"Jesus." June laughed, leaning forward to kiss Miriam again. "Forget I said anything. You're obviously a predator."

"Damn right." Miriam bit June's earlobe sharply before soothing it with her tongue. "Now take off your shirt."

June didn't want to think about how much that sentence turned her on. She pulled her cardigan and T-shirt off over her head, not caring that she was only in a boring white bra. The way Miriam looked at her made June feel delicious, the way Miriam touched her made June whimper.

"Christ, you're beautiful. Look at the size of those, they're practically spilling out." Miriam grabbed June's breasts with both hands, squeezing almost to the point of discomfort. After a moment, Miriam slid one hand inside June's bra, pinching at a large soft nipple.

"Knew you'd be like this," June gasped.

"Like what?"

"Sharp."

That startled a laugh out of Miriam, and she snapped her teeth against June's lips, sucking June's tongue back into her mouth. June could feel Miriam's hands now at the button of her jeans, feel slim fingers slip beneath the elastic of her underwear and slide between her legs.

"You're so wet. Is that just from me? Just from kissing me?"

June knew that she was wet, could feel herself clenching and unclenching with anticipation. Miriam's hand tugged June's pubic hair once before fluttering over her clit, circling her entrance. June wanted Miriam's fingers inside her. She wanted Miriam's tongue and Miriam's teeth.

"Or do you get like this for everyone? Just aching for someone to touch you." Miriam's tone was steady, but her voice broke slightly on the word "touch." "You seem the type."

"You don't even know me," June said, looking the other woman in the eye. She watched Miriam take her hand out of June's pants, drag those fingers over her tongue.

"I know what you taste like."

At this, Miriam toppled June sideways, stretching her out on her back against the couch. She was on June like a starving woman, pulling June's pants and underwear down her legs before diving forward, wrapping June's legs around her neck. Instantly June cried out at the feeling of Miriam's tongue against her, rougher and stronger and warmer than her hands. She couldn't help rocking her hips forward, seeking out more and more of the sensation. She was going to come. Just like this, with a stranger. She was going to come and it was going to be shattering.

"Please, fuck—please, please—"

"What do you want?" Miriam pulled that deadly mouth away, even though June cried out brokenly at the loss.

"Something—anything please, don't stop please—"

Again that tongue was back, but there were also fingers at her entrance. June couldn't tell how many as they slowly pressed inside her—two—no, three, four—too wide, too wide to take but she opened for them, arching her back as every part of her clenched and howled and came.

"Oh Jesus, oh—Jesus Christ don't stop!"

"You love it," Miriam whispered, barely audible over the roar in June's ears. "You love this."

She didn't give June a chance to recover, getting up from the couch and stepping out of her pants. Her underwear was pale pink silk as it fell to her ankles, her mound was blonde and trim, and her thighs were glistening. She climbed astride June and pulled June's hand between her legs, riding the slide of her fingers like she was wild. She rocked her hips over June's hand, never putting the fingers inside, only letting them stroke roughly over her again and again.

"You beauty," Miriam gasped. "You—gorgeous thing. Look at you."

June could imagine it, could see herself spread wide and flushed pink, sweat glistening across her collarbones. Miriam shone above her, blonde hair glowing like a halo as she rode June's hand.

"Make me come," Miriam ordered breathlessly, "Make me come, make me—"

Her voice cut off on a hard exhale and she squeezed her eyes shut, shaking against June's wrist. June watched her like there was nothing else in the world to see. She felt her body go white-hot at the flood of wetness against her hand, wanted to suck her fingers clean and then fuck herself on them.

Miriam fell forward, rested her head against June's chest. She breathed.

"How long before you can come again?"

"Predator," June laughed, and Miriam's hands were on her.

June walked home through the woods, messenger bag slung across her shoulder.

She felt like a sun that was rising.

HUSHER

Sommer Marsden

"I see you staring at her all the time," Maggie said. She nudged me with her elbow.

I glanced at her again. The girl with dark, dark hair wearing the black leggings and black Docs. I had come to think of it as her uniform. No matter the top she wore—tunic, sweater, hoodie, sweatshirt—she always had on the black leggings and Docs. I was curious to see if this fashion trend continued into the warmer months.

I shrugged, making an infused iced tea for the irritated soccer mom trying to get her toddler to stand up. Every time she let go of his hand, he dropped to the floor again. I tried not to smile. He seemed to be on a mission to make his mother nuts. My mother often claimed I had the same mission.

"Go talk to her already," Maggie hissed, putting a lid on the soccer mom's iced tea before bellowing her name: "Susan!"

Susan took the drink gratefully and hustled her apparently boneless child out of the coffee house.

"You do remember who *you're* talking to, right?" I snorted.

I wiped down the counter because we had an unexpected lull.

The black-uniformed girl ate her scone, sipped her plain black coffee, and read a book. I'd come to realize this was her lunch break.

Maggie rolled her eyes. "Yes, I realize. The world's shyest girl. But come on, Darby. Even you can muster up a little 'hi,' can't you?"

I shrugged.

"Ugh. Listen, I know someone who you know . . . " She leaned in close so I felt her breath on my ear. Maggie was cute, but not my type. "Had a little fling with her." Her eyes wandered pointedly to the dark-haired girl.

That perked me up. I cocked an eyebrow and stopped wiping the counter for a moment. "And?"

"And, you ask? Not who?"

I shook my head. "Nope. I don't care who it was. But I'd like to know how it was."

She rolled her eyes, clearly annoyed with my lack of curiosity on the identity of the person who fucked the dark-haired girl. "You're a weirdo, you know that?"

I nodded and waved my hand as if to say, go on . . .

Maggie grinned and spilled her guts. She apparently thought she had dirt. "She said it was good. Hot. Really hot, actually, but the girl was always telling her to hush. She was a husher, if you can believe it."

I giggled. "A husher?"

"Yeah, my friend said every time she'd try to talk while they were fucking, Angela would hush her."

"Angela," I said, letting the name roll off my tongue.

"Yes. Angela. By god, don't call her Angie, from what I hear."

I smiled. I wanted so badly to talk to this woman. The thought flitted through my head and as if she could hear me, she looked up and caught me staring. I looked away quickly, feeling fire fill my cheeks. Busted.

I went back to frantically wiping while my heart pounded

like a war drum. A moment later someone at the counter cleared her throat and I turned quickly, apologizing. "Sorry. I didn't see—"

It was her. She gave me a sarcastic little finger wave and a half smile. "Hey, there, stalker. What's your name?"

I thought my face was hot before; now it felt as if it'd burst into flames at any moment. My heart kicked in my chest. "I'm sorry I stared," I stammered. "I just . . . um . . . "

"Name?" she asked pointedly.

"Darby. My name is Darby."

"Are you always this talkative and smooth?" she asked.

A bark of laughter burst out of me and I clapped my hand over my mouth to silence myself. Then I took a deep breath and nodded my answer.

"Good. I think people talk way too much as it is. I know because I have bored women in my salon chair all day long. Then again, on the flip side," she pointed a finger at me. "When you find someone you'd like to listen to, it's pretty killer."

I nodded in agreement. My ex had always talked. She'd always wanted me to talk. She especially wanted me to talk dirty during sex, and my god, that was almost impossible. I went into myself during sex. I was focused on pleasure, getting it and giving it. I didn't want to chat.

She slid a card to me and said, "My number's on the back. Text me if you want to go out tomorrow. I can meet you here at six after my last cut."

She left without me having to say a word.

I watched her walk back to the salon and then disappear behind its mirrored doors.

Maggie came up behind me as I fingered the business card. "Dude . . . " she said.

"Yeah," I said.

* * *

I texted the number after I got home. I simply said: *I'd like to meet you after work tomorrow.*

What else could I say? But I was ridiculously grateful she'd said text and not call. My introverted self might have exploded in a fireball of panic had she said that.

The response came a moment later: *Cool. You like Chinese?*

I answered her and then went to take a long hot bath. I shut my eyes and inhaled the scent of lavender and bergamot. I would not, not, not stress over tomorrow, or play the scenario out in my head a thousand different horrible ways. Like me falling down, spilling my drink on her, calling her by my ex's name, or any other terrifying thing I could think up.

Instead, I'd focus on the fact that the universe had seen fit to drop her in my lap after so many months of watching her. Not too stealthily, I had been informed.

My fingers drifted down my thighs and I rubbed the aching muscles from being on my feet all day. It helped a little, along with the calming scent. Of course, her bright, gorgeous face popped up in my mind's eye. Her no-nonsense attitude. Her soft smoky voice. The thought of her hushing me while we were fucking. Literally, my dream come true . . .

My fingers drifted to my pussy and I figured what the hell. Go with it. Getting off was better than getting nervous.

I traced small soft circles on my clit and pleasure bloomed hot and pink in the very center of me. My hips bobbed up and I increased my tempo. Focusing on the image of her sweet Kewpie-bow mouth. On my mouth. On my throat, my shoulder . . . my nipple. I pushed a finger inside my cunt, imagining it was hers. I curled it softly against my G-spot. Then not so softly. I went back to my lovely wet circles and pictured her mouth between my thighs, sucking me, licking me . . .

Coming was sudden and sweet and I realized how hot it was in the tiny bathroom.

But at least I wasn't nervous.

She texted me before bed. Simply: *Goodnight, Darby.*

Goodnight, Angela.

I slept like the dead and then staggered through my workday. I got off at four, so I came home and took a shower before going back up to the store to meet her.

She was in her uniform of black leggings, combat boots, and a pop-culture tee with a big olive-green hoodie.

"Hungry?"

I cocked my head and stared at her mouth. My heart was pounding, but in a good way. "Yeah. I could eat."

She raised her eyebrows at me and gave me a half grin, but I didn't miss the bit of color that suddenly blossomed in her cheeks. I'd surprised her. That caused a bolt of pride and a swell of pleasure inside me. I was wet and bare beneath my jeans. The question of the night was, would she find that out? Because I knew one hundred percent that if she wanted to know, I'd show her.

At dinner, she talked about work a little and then stared me down. Those eyes of hers flashed dark-dark brown with hints of amber, like aged whiskey. "So, you're super talkative. Do you like being a barista?"

I nodded, swallowing the tiny bit of food I'd put in my mouth. The restaurant was small, dark, nearly empty, and the food was amazing.

"I do. For now. I wanted something that I could do while I work on my own stuff." I took another bite.

She stared at me for a moment and then burst out laughing. "And . . . your own stuff. That would be . . . ?"

"I make jewelry. I've been doing it for ages. Since the beginning of high school. I sell it online. It's growing."

She waited and I waited. "So, is every conversation going to be like pulling teeth?"

I smiled. "At first. I warm up."

"So, you're what? A super introvert? Horribly shy? Crippled by anxiety?" She touched the sterling silver ring on my pinky and a shot of excitement overtook me. My hand started to shake.

"I'm an introvert. I'm quiet. And I think before I speak. I do become chattier, but I'll never be a motor mouth."

She grinned. "Hey, Motor Mouth, did you make this?"

I nodded.

She stroked my finger. "Ever thought about fucking me?"

Somehow it didn't surprise me when she said it. But it did make my heart pound. I nodded again and swallowed my food before I choked.

"Want to leave this place and go to my place?"

Another nod.

She raised her finger to the waiter. "Can we get takeout containers, please?"

She dropped a twenty on the table and we left, hurrying out into the chilly evening wind like time was short. It wasn't short, but we were eager. On the way to her car, her fingers caught mine and she squeezed.

"You're quiet. I like that. When you speak, it means you have something to say."

I nodded, exhaled, felt a heady mixture of relief and gratitude rush through me. "Yes," I sighed.

Her apartment was nearly as tiny and dark as the Chinese restaurant. I had a fleeting moment to notice the interior and then she pushed me back against the wall, pressed her lean body against mine, and kissed me.

"Too fast?" she asked, when we came up for air.

I shook my head no and grabbed her collar and pulled her in.

How many times had I imagined this? Her warm against my body, her breasts pressed against mine, her lips on my lips.

Her hands settled on my waist and squeezed. I made a little sound but said nothing. Then I was lost in the sweetness of her tongue dancing over mine.

She moved her hands up beneath my sweater and I felt my skin pebble with goose bumps. Her fingers deftly unhooked the front clasp of my bra and then her warm hands were cupping my breasts, squeezing just enough for a shudder to roll through me. She felt it and then her fingertips were on my nipples, softly swirling the halos of flesh and then suddenly a pinch.

I yelped and she laughed. "Okay?"

I nodded again.

"Say yes," she said.

"Yes," I said. She smiled and grabbed a handful of my hair, tugging gently, pulling me in for another staggeringly good kiss.

I didn't say anything but I took her hand and pulled her toward the hallway. I was no detective but the lone hallway had to lead to a bedroom at some point.

Angela took the hint and took the lead. She pulled me to the second door on the left and I regarded her small room, whose contents included black futon, shocking purple tie-dyed wall hanging, and a stuffed bear the size of a small child. And not much else.

"He's mine from childhood. Not a word," she said, grinning.

I made the motion of locking my lips and tossed the imaginary key over my shoulder.

Then she was moving me to the bed, pushing me down, unbuttoning my jeans, and finding me bare beneath. "It's always the quiet ones," she said, laughing.

I smiled up at her and then tugged chunks of her dark-dark hair to get her closer. I kissed her, arching up, effectively pressing her palm to my shaved mound.

She made a pleased sound and got me out of my sneakers and jeans. I whipped off my top as she watched. She ran her hands over my tits, pinched my nipples. Her smile was secretive.

"And here I'd have thought you'd be all buttoned up. With maybe a matching white bra and panty set."

I shook my head and leaned up to tug at her leggings. She kicked off her boots and stripped as I watched. Black leggings, black socks, black panties, black sports bra.

Her uniform . . .

I snagged her wrist when she got close and pulled her down suddenly. I pushed her flat and climbed over her. Her dark eyes were wide as I leaned in to kiss her. "I thought I'd be—"

"On top?"

She nodded. I raked my teeth down her throat and over her collarbone. "We can take turns."

I was so grateful I didn't have to chatter, to talk and come up with dirty things to say, that I simply went with every impulse. My first being to drag my teeth over the twin protrusions of her hip bones.

She moaned, and I nipped the skin just above her mound. I pushed a finger inside her, feeling her warm wet cunt give me a welcoming clench. I slid my finger in and out, looking up to watch her pretty face as I touched her.

Her eyes drifted shut and her hips lifted. I added another finger and laid a proper kiss on her pussy. Not touching her clit, but coming so damn close.

"Jesus Christ!" Angela snarled.

A dark little chuckle slipped out of me as I curled my fingers deep inside her plush dampness.

"That was an evil little laugh for such an angelic-looking woman," she growled.

"Now you know my secret," I said. Then I nudged her clit with my tongue.

She grabbed a handful of my hair and tugged me closer. I lapped at her, and then flicked her clit fast and chaotic. She slammed up to meet my mouth. I went for it, slowly sliding a third finger inside her. I fucked her with my fingers and sucked her little clit hard over and over again.

When she came, she bellowed. She wasn't quiet and she wasn't shy. I wondered briefly about her neighbors and then realized I didn't care.

She sat up and pushed me hard. I went down on my back, my hair flying in my face. I found myself laughing, loud and uncontrollable. She seemed almost angry that I'd surprised her with my loudness in the bedroom as opposed to my quiet in public.

"Oh, you are gonna get it, little girl. Quiet but deadly in the sack, is that it? Shy but bold as balls?" She was grinning at me as she flipped me to my belly before I realized what she was doing. She was compact but she was strong. The muscles in her arms were lean and well defined. Her legs looked like she ran.

Her hand came down on my ass and the crack of the impact hurt my ears it was so loud. I bucked, cried out, and wanted to rub the sting. Then the endorphins kicked in as a warm thumping pleasure joined the already present arousal.

She shoved a finger in me and I gasped.

Her hand came down again. The moment I cried out, she wiggled that finger. She did it too many times for me to count and when my ass pounded like a heartbeat, she turned me over. I winced, wriggled.

"Does your bum hurt, love?"

Before I could nod, her lush mouth latched on to me and her tongue flicked my clit. I forgot how to talk and hissed instead. She dragged the tip of her tongue over me slowly. So slowly I could hardly stand it. Her fingers moved inside of me. Her mouth was hot and eager on my pussy.

Another slow, slow drag, and I thought I might die.

"Please—" I managed, moving restlessly. She flexed the finger in my cunt and I moaned. "Fuck. Please . . . "

She caved, moving her tongue in wonderful patterns. Sucking me hard and then soft and then simply swirling her tongue. The pressure built and built until I thought I'd die . . . or scream. Then she added a second finger and drove deep inside me.

I came. I came with a loud sob, my body dancing under her touch. I bucked and cried and she laughed before finally hushing me.

"Shh . . . " she said, curling up against me.

I hushed. I hushed gratefully. No chatter-chatter-chatter postsex.

She kissed my neck and said, "You surprised me, stalker."

I snorted by way of response.

"But in a good way," she said. "Hungry?"

"Starved!"

"Oh, now she talks!"

"I talk. I just . . . "

She nudged me with her elbow. "I get it. No need to explain. We can talk, we can not talk, as long as we can do that again . . . It's all good, stalker."

I looked up at her and traced her nipple with my fingertip. I watched it pebble beneath my touch. How many times had I imagined her in bed? So many it hurt my brain. Finally, I said, "Oh, we can do that as much as you want. I might even say a few words here and there."

"Be still my heart," she said.

FEARLESS

T. C. Mill

It was the kind of day when you could smell the sunlight. It poured down, warm rather than hot; the walk to the corner cafe had worked up a sweat, but a soft breeze dried it on Jenny's forehead, tugging her ponytail, pressing her thin T-shirt to her stomach or her jacket against her back depending on which direction they turned. Her shirt was damp enough at the neck to approach transparency, legs that had been cramped beneath a desk all week had started to feel floaty with exercise, and when Jenny closed her eyes she imagined the sun shining right through her as if she were as invisible as a window. Tessa's hand in hers was all that kept her from deliciously dissolving.

The sun drank up the remains of the rain from early that morning, but the grass remained springy underfoot when they cut across it. The air was scented with humidity rising off the green spaces, the baked denim on her shoulders, and water passing under the bridge. You could smell how cool that water was in its depths and shadows.

The river had risen overnight, almost swallowing the rocks in its bed. Jenny slowed to watch it flow, silver and so smooth that she thirsted to dip her hand in it. At the thought, her fingers folded, forming a light fist on one hand and squeezing Tessa's on the other. The water's sound was deeper, less the trickling chime it made in the middle of the summer drought and more of a hum, like the rumble that came from the billows of fabric swinging around Tessa's ankles with each step.

Jenny's eyes went to Tessa and stayed there.

First her sundress's skirt, which shaped itself to her legs with each stride forward. The fabric was burgundy with tiny white flowers and coiling green vines. A drawstring tightened the dress at her waist, and the cut-out shoulders revealed skin the sun had turned golden. Beneath her cream-colored hat, her hair was deep auburn, almost the color of port wine, black in the shadows. It was a color Jenny could taste, strong and sweet—and Tessa's skin, salt and tartness and honey on the flat of her tongue.

She reached up with her free hand and let the tips of her fingers be caught by Tessa's curls. They pulled free as Tessa turned her head, looking at Jenny over the rim of her sunglasses. Her eyes gleamed and her cherry lips quirked.

"You really can't resist?" she asked.

"Not even in public," Jenny admitted unapologetically. "I love your hair. Always will." She leaned closer and whispered, "You look too delicious not to touch."

Tessa squeezed her hand. The tip of her tongue passed over her lips teasingly.

A lamppost on the bridge forced them to pass one at a time, so Jenny dropped back to let Tessa walk ahead—keeping her view of wine red and sun honey gold. But Tessa's hat prevented her from seeing farther ahead, so the shouting came as a surprise.

It wasn't only loud, it was *trying* to be loud. Trying so hard that the words took on a hoarse edge, as if rusty. Jenny pictured a machine suddenly, a machine designed to do nothing but shout, loud and repetitive and relentlessly unstoppable. The sweat on her shoulders ran cold. Jenny didn't do well with raised voices.

What the guy said echoed weirdly down the streets, so she couldn't make out more than a few syllables here and there. Something about "repentance." And "sinners." And either becoming worthy or being unworthy, thoughts that always left her feeling equally unfit. Jenny didn't do well with that kind of thing, either.

Tessa glanced over her shoulder, steps slowing. Jenny's hand on hers had tightened to a death grip.

"Where is he?" Jenny asked.

"The preacher? Well, it's a group, sort of. At the corner of the park, right at the end of the bridge. They're handing out pamphlets, and, ugh. There are posters. Whoa—" She stopped entirely, wincing. But she didn't pull out of Jenny's hold.

"Let's cross the street."

Tessa looked next to them, at the parking lot the bridge had become as cars inched toward the Saturday market at the other end of the park. Except it wasn't quite a parking lot, because then the light on the other side changed and every vehicle lurched ahead, way too fast to duck between them safely.

"We can wait here," Jenny said.

"We can," Tessa said, "but we don't have to." She started walking again, slowly but deliberately, each step showing her legs against her skirt—muscular calf, full thigh, so gorgeous that even slogans about sin couldn't distract Jenny from her entirely. And she didn't let go of Jenny's hand.

They came closer to the voices.

Unable to shut her eyes, Jenny dropped them to the pavement in front of her feet. She wanted each word to pass right through her the way the sun felt it could, leaving no shadow. Instead she felt them, rusty-edged, hooking onto her. With every step the hooks got better traction. Once they came abreast of the speakers she imagined them pulling her away. Taking her back. Making her listen, and obey, and change from all she had grown into.

They didn't, somehow. She kept her eyes on Tessa, climbing from her ankles to her waist, up her spine to the sweet nape of her neck, not yet hidden by her growing hair. They were at the end of the bridge, almost before the crowd. It was very small. Jenny didn't look closer. She gravitated toward the opposite side of the narrow sidewalk, pulling Tessa's arm behind her back. Tessa glanced at her, sunlight slanting across her reflecting shades, but didn't let go of her hand, even if the position was uncomfortable. If she had let go, Jenny would have been comfortless; but she also would have been free to get away—across the street, even back the way they'd come.

And then they were past.

Heart pounding, breath short, Jenny stumbled along a few more paces. At least her nauseous anxiety was receding. But in its place came anger. The hand-holding made her feel like a child, but you were supposed to protect children. She *wasn't* a child, and god knew she didn't want Tessa to treat her like one, but some part of her felt helpless, betrayed. Still wishing she could have run.

She released Tessa's hand, slipping her own fingers free. As quietly as she could—not very—she said, "It's like you have no fucking concept of fear!"

Tessa didn't take it as a compliment. Tessa didn't take it at all. They walked in silence until Jenny swallowed the bitter taste in her mouth and said, "I'm—"

"Some things it doesn't pay to be afraid of." Tessa didn't sound upset with her for snapping, just a little tired. But her words, however mild, were a frank reminder.

"Yeah." They stopped at the corner, waiting for the light to change. Jenny didn't try to apologize again, and she didn't expect or need an apology from Tessa. After a few seconds, she admitted in a lighter tone, "And I was already nervous."

Tessa took her hand again. From the corner of her eye Jenny saw her smile. "Let's get home."

With the apartment door locked behind them, they started undressing. Tessa tossed her hat onto the table by the door and wiggled out of her sundress, shrugging her shoulders through the straps that had left them bare and twisting her arms in movements that were unself-consciously awkward. Jenny's heart ached as she watched, as if it was constricted in a cage almost too small to let it beat. Then Tessa let the dress fall around her feet and stepped out of it.

A tan showed on the caps of her shoulders and her arms, and then a little less brightly on her neck and the tops of her breasts. Below that, everywhere she was normally covered, her skin looked cool, pale, both voluptuous and vulnerable. The surgery scars were fading.

Jenny took a step toward her only to realize she still wore shoes. She kicked her feet out of them, then pulled off jacket, T-shirt, and jeans. Her stomach was cool with sweat, making the heat below even stronger. Her pulse beat between her legs as she approached Tessa.

When she was naked, Jenny always felt more powerful—paradoxically untouchable. It was almost as good as being transparent, like sunlit air, like water. She felt strong enough to say, "So . . . you want to do this?"

Smiling, Tessa reached for her.

"I know." Blushing, she continued with her apology: "But . . . *this?* We could try another day."

"I think we've waited long enough," Tessa said. "*I* have." She stepped closer, still with her arms out, bringing Jenny into them without closing them around her. "We've both seen much scarier things."

Jenny let out a breath so deep she shivered with it. Then she lifted her own arms, meeting Tessa's embrace.

When she was naked, Jenny became shockingly aware of how much *skin* she had, every inch of its surface alive with texture—the carpet under her feet, the warm air of the room, and of course, Tessa's skin. Jenny's fingers skimmed her wrist, were captured as Tessa turned her hand and pulled them up to her mouth, put her lips around the pads and nails, not quite sucking, not quite nibbling, but something like both. Jenny's free hand cupped the back of Tessa's head, moving lightly through her hair.

She couldn't resist it, always loved it—in some ways she now loved it even more. It had grown in darker after the chemo, thicker, with more curl to it, and was one of the most visible signs of her recovery.

That, and the fact that getting frustrated, snapping, falling apart was something Jenny only let herself do now that Tessa was recovered.

Tessa had never had the stereotypical redhead temper, but she'd become quieter since. Some of it had been exhaustion—she got frustrated, but didn't have the energy for rage. And after getting through that, she simply seemed calmer. As she'd told Jenny, it had been a change in perspective, one they were still finding their way around.

She stroked down Tessa's neck, around her shoulders, coming down to her tan lines. As she skimmed the tops of her breasts, Tessa sighed, breath fluttering around Jenny's fingertips.

Jenny cupped one of them. "Is this okay today?"

"Yes. Harder." Tessa clasped Jenny's hand and squeezed it tighter.

After her surgery and reconstruction, the nerve endings were tender sometimes. They'd learned to take it day by day. And now Tessa's breasts were more sensitive around the sides and at the top, high up. As Jenny gripped and massaged her, she also bent her head to trace her mouth over the start of Tessa's cleavage, then even farther up toward her neck. Tessa sighed, tipping her face back as Jenny started nipping.

The nips became harder, as did her hold on Tessa's breasts, stronger and firmer as Tessa pressed close, her legs spreading to fit Jenny between them. "Like this," she murmured. "Keep going. You're not going to break me."

No, she wasn't. Tessa loved how she made love to her, Jenny knew, because Jenny was the one person willing to treat her as if she were unbreakable. Even though everyone was breakable. They'd never forget that. Yet here Tessa stood—swaying a bit on her feet, but holding her ground—open and unafraid.

Jenny hummed against her neck, paused for a gentle kiss before continuing with a soft but unhesitant nip. It felt good. She had always loved to bite, squeeze, palm—to take, as if having someone else could help to fill the hollowness where she was scared.

She tried to do better. But sometimes it rose up, sickening and nearly paralyzing. It was her worst nightmare to be made a helpless child again. To be up against a force she couldn't evade or bargain with. To lose what was precious to her, unspeakably precious, like a toy confiscated because she didn't deserve it.

"Hey," Tessa said. She must have noticed Jenny's distraction in a slip of her hands. "Hey." She held her shoulders without stepping back.

"I know," Jenny said. "Some things it doesn't pay to be afraid of."

"It doesn't. Not after you've done all you can."

Jenny remembered Tessa's hands moving over her breasts, a routine check made more than routine by experience. The pads of her fingers traced circles, soft then firm, a touch that was caring rather than sexual but arousing too in its tenderness. And today, those same fingers entwined with hers, holding her as they walked together.

Then Tessa shrugged, a quick, thin smile darting across her face. "Anyway, what really fucks everything up will be something you never expected."

Jenny laughed with her. The gallows humor was another new development, and maybe an alternative to anger—hints of irony had come to full flower in waiting rooms and under chemo drips, thoroughly fertilized by Jenny's own sardonic outlook. When they'd first become a couple she'd tried to curb it for Tessa's sake. An attempt to protect her, she realized now. Pointless and unnecessary, in the end.

She was only a year younger than Tessa, who as every doctor had commented, was herself "so young." Jenny felt less wise, less experienced, and of course the cancer had only widened that gap. Yet as Tessa pointed out, she didn't have Jenny's history, either. They both survived. They both had parts that needed to be handled carefully, day by day—but not too gently, not so skittishly they seemed easily breakable. And they could share both strength and vulnerability.

Jenny knelt, letting her kisses travel down to Tessa's stomach. Then lower, lips skimming her thighs. Her hands wrapped around Tessa's hips and legs. She squeezed her ass too, and Tessa sighed roughly in satisfaction. Sometimes Jenny would grip her tightly enough to leave light scratches, but not today—her nails had been filed so close their tips were pink. It'd be worth it.

She nudged, directing Tessa toward the bed. In this small room, it wasn't far to go. She stood as Tessa took the necessary step.

Tessa spread out her arms, not to catch herself but to pull Jenny with her as she tumbled onto the bed. They rolled over each other, wrapping together, kissing and laughing and gasping for breath, sheets tangling around their feet until they kicked them away.

From the storage bin under the mattress, Jenny pulled out a vial of massage oil, then a pump jar of lube. Tessa lay back, resting on her elbows.

"I want you so much," she said.

Jenny wasn't eloquent at moments like these, struck speechless by the gorgeous body spread naked on their bed, words drying in her mouth with emotion. "Me too," she said at last. "I mean, you too. I want you. Here."

She knelt between Tessa's spread legs, pouring the oil over her fingers first. They glided over Tessa's shoulders and breasts, circling the reconstructed nipples before sweeping back up to trace her collarbone. Muscles in her neck and shoulders relaxed under Jenny's touch. The warmth of Tessa's skin sent up the lavender scent of the oil.

"That's . . . so good . . . " Tessa was also becoming ineloquent, seeming to melt under the massage. Slowly, she turned over so Jenny could work down her back. "Yes . . . lower . . . "

She kept her legs wide, and Jenny playfully went over her butt, slipping a finger into her cleft and stroking along it. But she didn't penetrate her anally, or go any farther forward. They had other plans.

She worked on Tessa's thighs until they went silken and then started turning taut again from anticipation and arousal. Jenny traveled along her spine, sliding over her body, half lying atop her with a leg slipped between hers. Tessa rocked against the pressure.

"I'm ready, Jen. Whenever you are."

"I was ready when I woke up this morning." Jenny kissed her shoulder before Tessa flipped over again. "Don't know why you insisted on exercise *before* the exercise."

"Because if we didn't get some fresh air this morning, there's no way we'd get any later. Do you plan on leaving this bed before tomorrow?"

"Maybe for refreshment."

"There's water here."

A carafe of water waited on the bedside table—a beautiful crystal jar that was one of Tessa's antiquing finds—and Jenny nodded, even though she was mildly annoyed with herself for not refreshing it from the Brita pitcher in the fridge.

"It's thirsty work." She trailed her lips and hands down Tessa's torso. "Mouthwatering too."

She kissed the edge of the landing strip of dark hair while her fingers slipped between Tessa's labia. She was wet; not as much as she used to be—another reason cancer blew, as if they needed one more—but silky under Jenny's touch, and the rich smell of her rose, even better than lavender.

Jenny couldn't keep her other hand away from her own clit, at least for a few strokes, rubbing brief and hard over flesh gone rigid with the excitement building as she explored Tessa's body.

If she kept it up, she wasn't far from coming. She loved clitoral stimulation—direct, firm, often easy, and sometimes even too quick. Tessa, on the other hand, preferred to be filled. Her G-spot was dynamite, or maybe Vesuvius. They'd both been counterintuitive for each other at first, and spent some time apologetically explaining how they worried they were "weird." And then they spent a lot of time enjoying versatile configurations—Jenny riding Tessa's thigh while fingering her, or the wonderful weekend they'd spent with their first strap-on.

Above all, though, Tessa loved her fingers.

Lots of them.

Jenny slipped the tip of one in, gliding just on Tessa's wetness. She sank into that hot, tight grip. Both of them caught their breaths audibly.

"The light's definitely green for more." Tessa reached for the bottle of lube and thrust it down at her.

Jenny pumped some onto her hand, then let the bottle fall beside them on the mattress, knowing she'd want more of it later. Her first two fingers slipped inside Tessa smoothly, eased by the lube and her arousal. She stroked in and out, a little deeper each time, rubbing the muscular walls and feeling them quiver and relax around her.

She started with a third finger, but Tessa murmured, "Yellow" and she added more lube first, then concentrated on more stroking and circling. At last it made its way in, the tightness a little hotter, each small motion more exciting.

They'd gotten this far before, but the fourth finger could be tricky, and the thumb . . . well, this was the first time trying to go all the way since Tessa entered remission. And even before then, it wasn't an everyday thing.

"After more than a year," she had said last night, "I am so seriously ready to feel your fist in me."

Jenny had been speechless in response to that too.

It felt so good to sink into her now—to dip her hand in the river of her, warmer than the sun, sweeter than wine. Jenny tucked her pinkie against her ring finger and felt Tessa draw her in, a gentle, gradual welcome home. She turned her hand slowly, hearing Tessa sigh, hearing the stir of wetness where they connected. She had to pause to manage her own breathing. She'd forgotten to do it for a few seconds.

Her pulse was jumping in her chest and behind her clit. It fluttered like a caged bird, not just from anxiety but from exhilaration, ready to take flight. She brought her other hand to Tessa's chest, having to stretch a bit because of her girlfriend's height. Tessa tried to wiggle down to meet her, drawing her legs farther up, letting Jenny's fingers move a little deeper inside her.

Jenny rubbed the slopes of her breasts, bending every so often to kiss her navel and the edges of her slit. "You're so fucking gorgeous," she said. "This feels amazing. For me. Does this feel amazing for you?"

"Of course it does," Tessa said, but her laughter wasn't mocking—instead it was half a moan of pleasure, half a gasp at the thrill. "You're gorgeous too, Jenny. I love looking up at you from this angle—your hair's got the blue highlights today, did you know? Maybe it's the sunlight . . . and goddess, the things your arm muscles do when you fuck me."

Jenny didn't think of herself as having especially impressive arm muscles, but what Tessa was talking about happened when she worked them like this—not extreme gestures but focused tension, a small flexing beneath the surface of her skin that you'd have to be watching very closely to see. And Tessa was. *And she thought it was gorgeous.*

"Also," Tessa said, "I'm green for another finger, if you are."

Jenny smiled. "I'm out of fingers."

"You mean . . . ?"

She passed her thumb across Tessa's labia, rolling it gently over her clit, then folded it to join the rest of her hand at her entrance. Jenny pressed her fingers into a star shape, narrow as she could make it, and added more lube.

"I'm green for this," Tessa said, but slowly, reverently, as if she couldn't fully believe it herself.

"You're doing awesome," Jenny said, her own voice hushed in awe. "Let me know if you want to try something different."

She moved into her. Reached into her. Slid into her, a key into a lock. Not easily—nothing so overwhelming could be easy—but fearlessly.

Tessa cried out.

"Are you—"

"Green! Please . . . "

At first she only held in place, appreciating their achievement. After months of slowly working up to it, she had found her place inside Tessa again. She fit her as she always had—tighter, but slick from the lube and honeyed with her juices and warm and right.

Then Jenny moved her fingers slightly, stroking for her G-spot. It was obvious when she found it. Tessa was always a responsive lover, but not always big on volume. Now, though, they could probably hear her across the state line—and Jenny adored the idea.

She kept flexing her curved hand, feeling the familiar rough tissue against the pads of her fingers, wet heat against her skin, the close grip all the way to her wrist. Then came the ripples of Tessa's orgasm. Jenny stopped moving, letting it happen, feeling it happen. Her girlfriend's strength stole her breath, like always. An expression swept across her face like a summer thunderstorm. Jenny watched, vision blurry, and realized she was crying herself. Happy tears. She licked a salty drop from the corner of her mouth.

With her fingers relaxed, slick, squeezed, it felt as if Jenny had let go of something . . . and somehow the exact opposite, all at once. As if she were being given a gift so precious it couldn't be physically held.

Eventually, Tessa nodded, and Jenny began to pull out, adding a little more lube to ease the way. When suction made it tricky, she slipped the finger of her opposite hand in alongside her wrist to help break it. *Suction, not wrist.* The thought and the feeling as she was released were both kind of funny, but her heart felt squeezed as tightly as her hand had been at another realization— Tessa's body didn't want to let her go.

Once she was free, she stretched her fingers, curled them in a tight fist, and unfurled them again. They gleamed with Tessa's juices, and she couldn't resist licking them. Tessa moaned at the sight.

Jenny made herself get out of bed to pour water for both of them, and as she turned around, it was her turn to moan. Tessa lay in the middle of the mattress, flushed, shining with sex, the sheets crumpled and stained around her. She grinned up at Jenny, blissed out, barely able to move. But after emptying the glass Jenny held to her lips, she said, "Here. Want you. I want to taste you."

Kneeling beside her on weak knees, Jenny felt dizzy, ready to fall. But she straddled Tessa's body, moved over her, bracing her hands on the wall above the pillows. Tessa's hands climbed up her legs, came to her waist, pulled her down to meet her mouth.

She flicked her tongue over the pearl of her erect clit. Jenny sighed and rotated her hips to meet her licking. Then, with sudden ferocious playfulness, Tessa caught her between her teeth—her unfaltering, unhesitant, loving teeth. It was a gentle hold but undeniable. Jenny's breath caught. Her most tender flesh, already alive in every nerve, seemed to catch fire from the intensity, not the sensation alone but the idea of it.

She felt herself there.

She let herself trust.

And then with another flick of the tongue, she was released, sliding free. A rush of blood filled her, and another sweep of pleasure as Tessa sipped at her salt-honey-tartness, warm as the sun, shook through her body and ignited. She flew into bliss.

Not invulnerable, but fearless nonetheless.

THE NIGHT SHIFT

Pascal Scott

"Thank you for calling Western North Carolina Adventures," Angel says in her sweet voice.

Some callers expect to hear a Southern drawl when they reach us and are disappointed by anything else. Angel has yet to lose the Manila accent that marks her as "not from around here." But Angel is a good employee—conscientious and dedicated. I'm not going to discriminate just because she doesn't talk like a local.

Angel is my latest hire. She's twenty-two and newly married to a native-son soldier, which is how she ended up here in North Carolina from the Philippines. From what I've observed, Angel is a very *young* twenty-two, innocent and unsophisticated by American standards.

"How may I help you this early morning?" Angel continues, politely.

I'm listening in my office on my headphones. I've got my checklist in front of me, making sure Angel hits her marks. Check one is for thanking the caller: one point. Check two for asking to help.

Another point. But she forgot to tell the caller her name. I've got to dock her for that, two points off.

The caller seems hesitant, taking a breath before she answers in a low, throaty voice, almost a whisper.

"You sound nice," the caller says.

Angel doesn't miss a beat.

"Thank you," Angel replies, brightly. "May I have your name?"

Check three. Get the caller's name. Another point.

"Samantha," the caller responds. "Call me Sammy."

"Thank you, Mrs. Sammy. How may I help you this early morning?"

Check four, repeat the name. Use a formal title: Mrs. until she says otherwise if the caller is female. Another point.

"It's not Mrs.," Samantha corrects. "But call me Sammy. Please."

"Thank you, Sammy," Angel goes on. "What may I do for you this early morning, Sammy?"

"I was hoping you could talk to me for a little while," Sammy says, her tone becoming more confident but remaining low and smoky.

I hear the slight slur of alcohol on Sammy's tongue and check the shiny white face of the wall clock in my office—2:40 a.m. Adventures always seem like a better idea at 2:00 a.m. than they do, say, eight hours later.

We give our agents three minutes to hook the caller or they lose points. That's not a lot of time. Lose enough points or fail to make the minimum, and you're fired. Corporate's rules, not mine. Our sales pitch is simple. Life is stressful, but not here in the mountains. Here you can escape your worries for a few days or a few weeks just by booking a stay at one of our three properties in Western North Carolina. Pick your adventure: mountain climbing, white-water rafting, hiking, gem hunting, zip lining, or try our sample package that includes a little of everything.

Angel continues.

"Yes, Sammy, I'd be happy to talk to you," she says quickly. "What might you be interested in this early morning?"

"I'll get to that in a minute," Sammy responds. "But first, tell me *your* name."

"My name is Angel."

I add a point back because Angel did it—she gave her name—although she had to be prompted.

"Angel," Sammy repeats. "That's a pretty name. You sound pretty. Pretty and petite. Are you pretty and petite, Angel?"

"Why yes I am," Angel says, ingenuously. "How did you know?"

I put down my pencil and tear off my headset. In another moment I'm out of my office and bounding the six long strides it takes me to reach Angel's cubicle. Spotting a yellow Post-it note pad on her desk I use a WNCA-branded ballpoint pen to scribble an urgent message. *PUT HER ON HOLD,* the note says.

Angel looks at me with wide-open, dark eyes.

"Excuse me for one moment, Sammy," she says into her mouthpiece. "My supervisor is asking me to put you on hold."

I wait while she listens to something Sammy is telling her.

"No, I won't . . . " Angel says pleasantly to Sammy before hitting the HOLD button and turning to me with an expression of bewilderment and protest.

"Angel," I say slipping into my older-and-wiser, I'm-in-charge voice. "I'm going to go back to my desk now and when I get there I'll call you, and then I want you to transfer that caller, Sammy, back to me. Can you do that?"

Angel is a Millennial. Of course she can do that.

"No problem," she answers, using her favorite American tag line.

"Good," I say. "I'll take this one and then you can take the next call that comes in."

"Oh," she says, clearly disappointed.

"This wasn't a call for you," I tell her.

As I walk back to my desk, I'm thinking, *no, not a call for you at all.*

After the call center went 24/7, Corporate assigned me to the worst shift, 11:00 p.m. to 7:00 a.m. No reason was given but I knew—Corporate doesn't like queers. Here in North Carolina we LGBT folk don't have legal protection in the workplace, and employers can discriminate any way they choose.

To climb the management ladder at WNCA you have to be the right age, race, gender, religion, and sexual orientation. I'm a fifty-three-year-old, lapsed-Catholic lesbian. That's why I'll never be more than a low-level supervisor with a closed door and a closet-size office in the basement, working the witching hours. I made supervisor at all just because turnover in the call center is so high, between seventy and eight-five percent during any given season. I'm the only one who has stuck around. The Millennials don't stay because they get bored and want to try something new. Gen Xers find better-paying jobs. The Boomers can't handle the technology.

I stay because of inertia. I've worked for WNCA for the last ten years and, unless I win the Powerball, I doubt I'll leave any time soon. My paycheck is enough to cover a rented room in a gay household, food and beer, and Saturday nights on a bar stool nursing a whiskey at Scandals, our local queer dance club. At this point in my life, that's all I really need—except maybe a girlfriend. But on my salary and at my age, romance doesn't seem to be happening. I've pretty much given up hope. I haven't had sex in longer than I care to admit.

Back in my office I close the door, put on my headset, and press a button on my phone system to complete Sammy's transfer to me.

"Thank you for calling Western North Carolina Adventures," I say in my most professional tone. "This is Alexis. I'm the supervisor here in the call center. How may I help you this early morning?"

"*Who* is this?" Sammy asks.

"My name is Alexis. I'm the supervisor in the call center of Western North Carolina Adventures. You were speaking a few minutes ago to one of my agents, Angel. I'm hoping I can help you. What can I do for you this early morning, Sammy?"

"*Where* am I calling?" Sammy asks, sounding genuinely perplexed.

"Western North Carolina Adventures," I repeat, more slowly. "May I ask what number you called to reach us?"

"Sure. Let me find it . . . Here it is. Nine hundred eight seven seven zero six one six."

I press the recording OFF button on my phone system to make sure that no one will ever hear this conversation except Sammy and me. I'm in my cinderblock office with the door closed and a Do Not Disturb sign hanging on the outside knob. My staff is on the phones. Corporate left hours ago.

"Yeah," I say, relaxing now. "I know what happened. You dialed *eight* hundred eight seven seven zero six one six by mistake. It's happened before. This is Western North Carolina Adventures. We're a tourist destination. I think you were trying to reach a *sex line*."

There's a long silence.

"Oh my god," Sammy says at last, breaking into a coughing laugh. I hear her take a loud gulp of something before she speaks again. "I am *so* sorry."

"Oh, it's happened before, believe me," I assure her. "The one you didn't reach is a sex line out of Greensboro. They recruit a lot of their employees from the university, I hear. We're here in Altamont, in the mountains. Where are you calling from?"

"Boone," she answers.

"Another university town. You work at the college?" I ask.

"No, I'm unemployed at the moment. Laid off. I drove a fork-lift for Foote Industries for twenty-three years before they went Chapter Eleven."

"Wow," I say. "Too much of that going on these days."

"Yah," she agrees.

"*Yah?*" I repeat. "What's the accent?"

"What do you mean?"

"*Yah.* We say *yeah* or *hell yeah* here in the South."

She laughs again.

"Foote Industries moved me to Minneapolis when the plant relocated there in '02. That's where I picked it up, probably. Naw, I'm homegrown. I'm from Boone. How about you? Are you from Altamont?"

"Hell no," I say. "I'm a Cali girl. Born and raised."

"How'd you get to the mountains?"

I sigh.

"Long story. The short version is this is where the van broke down. Girlfriend went back to LA. I stayed."

"Yah," she says. "I mean yeah. It happens."

"Usually we get men calling that line, men who have misdialed," I say, reflecting. "I think this is the first time we've ever had a woman caller."

"Really?" Sammy asks. "Well, I guess this is a night for firsts then."

"I suppose it is," I comment. And then I consider what she's just told me.

"So are you saying you haven't done this before? Called a sex line?"

"No, I haven't," she admits. "And isn't it just like me to dial up the wrong number?"

"Sounds like something I'd do," I tell her.

"Have you ever?" she asks, her tone lightening.

"What? Dialed a sex line by mistake?"

"No, you know what I mean. Called a sex line. Not by mistake."

I adjust my swivel chair so that I'm facing the blank wall. The fluorescent ceiling light bounces off the whiteness. I switch on a desk lamp and turn off the overheads.

"No," I say. "I haven't. I've never really considered it. It's sort of like thinking about finding a call girl for the night. You know, if you're a lesbian your mind just doesn't really go there."

"You're a lesbian?" she asks, more interested.

"Uh-huh," I say, although my head is still back on the idea of hiring a prostitute for the night.

"Not that there's anything wrong with wanting to hook up with a call girl," I elaborate. "A sex worker, I guess I should say. Or calling a sex line, either."

"Yah, but you do feel funny about it," she replies. "I mean, I do. You wouldn't believe how many shots I needed before I worked up the nerve to dial that number tonight. And then of course don't you know I dialed the wrong number. Blame it on Jack Daniels."

"Ah, Jack Daniels. I've spent some lonely nights with Mr. Daniels myself," I say.

Now why did I tell her that? I wonder for a quick moment before I remember that sometimes it's easier to confide in a stranger than it is in a friend. There's something seductive about anonymity whether it's in the confessional booth or the closet. That's why people have sex with strangers, which I've done a time or two myself.

"So what were you expecting tonight when you called the sex line?" I ask.

I kick off my new leather penny loafers. They're not broken in yet and a little stiff, especially the left one. I pull my left foot up, cross my ankle over my knee, and massage the toes. I work the ball of my foot and up to the heel.

"I don't know," she says. "I didn't know what to expect."

"Do they really ask what you're wearing?" I wonder aloud. "That's what you always hear. '*What are you wearing?*'"

She laughs. "I guess," she says.

My eyes wander down to what I'm wearing. It's the *opposite* of sexy. I've got on the WNCA uniform: a green polo shirt with the company logo on the right sleeve, khaki pants, and mud-brown socks and penny loafers.

"All right," I say, making an executive decision. "I'll play along. Let's pretend you've just called a sex line—"

"Well, I did just call a sex line, at least I meant to call a sex line—"

"And you've reached the sexiest woman on the planet. *Me.*"

"Hmm," Sammy says. "That sounds interesting."

I slip my voice into a lower register.

"Thank you for calling Nine Hundred SLUT. My name is Roxy. What may I do for you tonight?"

"Hey, you're good," Sammy tells me, surprised. "I like that voice."

"Thank you, baby. What's your name? And may I call you baby?"

"Sammy. And you may call me anything you like."

"Sammy," I say, "I like your attitude. I can tell you're a woman who knows what she wants and what Sammy wants tonight is an adventure. Sammy, I can assure you that you've reached the right girl."

"I believe I have," Sammy replies.

"Have you done this before, Sammy? Called us?"

"No, I haven't," she answers.

"Then you're a virgin. You're lucky you reached me, Sammy, because Roxy *loves* adventure virgins."

"She does? You do?" she asks.

"I do. What kind of adventure is Sammy interested in tonight? Mound climbing? Pearl diving? Maybe you're the kind of woman who likes water sports—"

"Whoa, are you sure you haven't done this before?"

"Never you mind all that, baby. Maybe I have, maybe I haven't. One thing I'll tell you, Miss Roxy is here now to take care of Sammy."

"All right, all right. Uh, maybe pearl diving. Maybe I'd like to dive down and find *your* pearl."

"Ooo, Sammy. That sounds just lovely. Maybe my pearl is wet right now. Maybe my pearl is just waiting for a big strong tongue to find its shell and pry it open and suck it out."

There's a long moment of complete silence.

"Sammy? Did I lose you, Sammy?"

"Uh, no. I was just . . . "

"Just what? Now Sammy, tell me. Do you have a finger on *your* pearl?"

"Uh . . . "

"Because if you don't, that's exactly what I want you to do right now. Will you do that for me, Sammy? Put your finger on your pearl?"

"Uh, yah."

I hear the sound of a zipper going down.

"Good. Now close your eyes and slip your hand between your legs and find that pearl. Because while you're doing that I'm going to crawl up that wonderful body of yours. Do you like long hair, Sammy?"

"Yah."

"That's good because I've got waves and waves of long, black hair. I'm going to lean down and let my hair brush against your naked breasts. I'm going to let the strands tease your nipples until they're hard for me. Do you think you'd like that, Sammy?"

"Uh, yah."

"Now I'm going to climb up a little higher until my pussy is over your face. Can you feel my pussy hovering over your face, Sammy? Can you smell me?"

I hear a gulp. This time she's not drinking.

"Uh-huh."

"Now keep your eyes closed, Sammy, and keep those fingers working your pearl. I'm going to lower my pussy down onto your mouth. I'm going to press my pussy lips against your lips. You're going to open your mouth and let your tongue find my pearl."

"Ohhh," Sammy moans.

"You remember what pussy tastes like, don't you, Sammy?"

"Umm-hmm."

"Sweet and salty and—"

"Oh god," Sammy groans. "Oh god, oh god, oh—"

"Sammy? Sammy? You still with me, Sammy?"

"Uh, yah," Sammy says, her voice cracking.

"Did you just come?" I tease.

"I did," she confesses in a gravelly voice.

"That was quick, girl," I say in my normal tone.

I hear the sound of her zipper pulled up.

"That was hot," Sammy says.

"Yes, it was."

And it was. I realize it *was* hot. Sometimes you pass on a woman because you're not attracted to her appearance. Maybe she's a big girl, and you have a thing for petite bodies. Maybe she has red hair and you like blondes. Maybe she's butch and you only go for femmes. Sometimes you miss a hot encounter because your biases get in the way. Maybe an anonymous call in the dark is just what you need to be reminded that all women have the potential to be sexy as fuck.

"It's getting late . . . " Sammy says, quietly.

"Yeah, I should let you go. I've got four more hours until I get off work."

She pauses.

"Maybe we can do this again? In person?"

Oh hell. *Why not?*

"Sure," I say. "That might be even hotter. And maybe we can slow things down next time. Make it last a little longer."

"Yah," she agrees. "Yeah, I mean. So, how about Saturday night?"

What? And tear myself away from my solitary bar stool at Scandal's?

"Saturday night," I confirm. "Call me. You've got my number."

"Yes I do," she says.

"Good night, Sammy."

"Good night, Roxy."

At shift's end my agents and I log out and hang up our headsets. It's 7:00 a.m. as the morning crew comes on to sell anonymous callers another day of adventures in the mountains. In the narrow stairwell, Angel stops me before I open the heavy exit door.

"Did you take care of Miss Sammy?" Angel wants to know.

I check twice, but I see nothing in her dark eyes but youthful innocence.

"Yes, Angel," I tell her. "I took care of Miss Sammy."

THE AUCTION

R. G. Emanuelle

Gia ambled around the room, looking at the hors d'oeuvres, the art on the walls, and the dresses on the women. Very little caught her interest, with the exception of the women.

These ladies were turned out to the ultimate in their little black dresses, beautifully coiffed hair, and perfect makeup complete with lush false eyelashes. Legs that never seemed to end . . .

She shook her head and took a sip of champagne. Most of these women were straight. Except that some of them weren't. She'd heard that this fundraising auction would be quite different than others. Gentlemen were being auctioned off, but a few women were going to be auctioned off as well. *To other women*, which was the important part. That was the only reason Gia had agreed to come. That and the promise of booze.

Of course, she'd never have the nerve to bid on any of them. But she wanted to watch. What kind of women would they auction off? What kind of women would bid on them? And how much?

The auction was late getting started. Delays over this and that, she'd overheard. Who cared? She was bored and she wanted to get on with it.

A server was making her way toward her with a tray of empty glasses. She knocked back the rest of the champagne in her glass, and placed it on the tray skillfully as it passed, without missing a beat. She picked up another glass from a table, where a bartender was filling more flutes. The bartender was a cute brunette, her longish brown hair tied back professionally. Her red vest was tight around her breasts and Gia couldn't help tracing them with her eyes—

Stop it! She turned around quickly. God, she was acting like a horny teenager. It was only when she'd reached a certain age that she came to believe what she'd been warned about—her hormones would explode and she'd want to fuck anything that moved.

The music stopped and the crowd hushed down. *Finally.* After a good slug of her drink, she made her way toward the staging area. The large turnout meant standing room only for the bidding. That was a good strategy. The energy was higher when everyone stood.

The mistress of ceremonies, a middle-aged socialite whose claim to fame was fundraising, stepped up to the mike, looking quite comfortable in her silver sequined evening dress and Sergio Rossi shoes.

"Good evening, ladies and gentlemen. I'm Muffy Pendleton. Welcome to this year's charity auction. This year, we're spicing things up. There will be bachelorettes up for bid."

At the sound of males voicing approval, Muffy added, "Just for the ladies, though. This is ladies' night, after all," she said, with a rich-bitch smile and a wag of her finger. "Yes, we are broadening our horizons, and why not? It's especially appropriate because half of this year's proceeds are going to benefit homeless LGBT youth."

This was met with cheers and whistles.

"All right, without further ado, let's start the auction!"

Whooping and hollering was soon drowned out by music.

"Our first bachelor . . . " Muffy went on to espouse the wonderful qualities of about six men.

The champagne was hitting Gia hard by now, and as if her hormones weren't fucking with her enough, the alcohol chimed in. She even looked at some of the guys with interest. A nice broad chest . . . a pretty face . . .

Ugh, stop it!

Worse, Muffy Pendleton was starting to look good to her. She had a nice pair of tits. Pour some tequila down her throat and she was probably wild in bed.

Ahhhhh!

"And now, for our Sapphic sisters in the house tonight . . . "

Oh, brother. Or should it be oh, sister?

" . . . we now present our bachelorettes."

Okay, here we go. Gia perked up, her little champagne haze settling down as she watched three women being auctioned off. The first one was very feminine-looking, with long blonde hair cascading down her back, and her neckline dropping so low it was more like a navel line. Gia wished she had the nerve to bid on her, because she really, really just wanted to run her tongue between and around her breasts.

The second woman was an African American woman in a slinky dark-purple gown that hugged every curve. It had a slit all the way up to her hip. Wildly sexy. She couldn't have been wearing a bra, judging from the protruding nipples. Very suckable.

The third woman was the butchy type. She wore a smart Armani suit, highly polished oxford shoes, and her hair was short and slicked back. Very cool and self-assured. Her face was masculine but soft at the same time, and she had an athletic build. She could probably fuck all night.

Oh, Christ on a cracker. Sweat began to bead on Gia's forehead and she wiped it with her little cocktail napkin, which promptly shredded into thin, tight ropes. She looked around for a place to toss it and found a service table by the side of the room. As she went toward it, Muffy announced the fourth, and last, woman to be auctioned.

The bachelorette walked out, a shy little smile on her face, and sauntered to center stage. Neither feminine nor masculine, but somewhere in between, she had short black hair cropped close at the sides, and wore a suit with a white shirt opened to her cleavage. Muffy spoke, but Gia heard none of it. Her stomach flipped over and turned inside out, and her pulse beat hard in her throat. She sliced her way back to the front.

Gia's head snapped back and forth as women bid on the bachelorette, higher and higher. The frenzy of the bidding must have penetrated her brain because, almost against her volition, her hand went up, her mouth opened, and the words "four hundred" came tumbling out.

What the hell was she doing?

"Four hundred. Do I hear four-fifty?" Muffy called out. "Yes, four-fifty to the lady in the back."

"Five," Gia shouted. Some alien—a rich alien—had taken over her mouth.

Gia heard "Five-fifty!" from somewhere in the back of the room. Gia suddenly found herself in a bidding war with an unknown person over a stranger. Then, Gia said, "Eight hundred."

Muffy waved a well-manicured finger around the audience. "Do I hear eight-fifty? No? Eight hundred to the lady in front in the smart Donna Karan suit."

Applause surrounded Gia as her stomach tightened and her ears rang. What had she done? She suddenly felt as if she were in a vortex—all sound muffled and all visuals blurred.

"Winning bidders, please go to the registrar's desk to pay for your prizes," Muffy said, with a little too much pleasure.

With a slight tremor in her knees, Gia made her way to the registrar. After giving her name and the auction number, she pulled her credit card out of her purse and handed it to her.

The registrar handed back her card, along with an envelope. "In there, you'll find instructions on how to claim your prize," she said.

Eww. She made it sound so tawdry. These things probably just ended up being friendly dinners, and that's it. After all, the people being auctioned off weren't prostitutes.

Were they?

No, of course not. They were nice people who put themselves in an awkward position for a good cause.

She slipped the envelope in her purse and looked around for more champagne and food. She needed to fortify herself.

"Congratulations."

Gia turned to see a redheaded woman in an expensive-looking dress and shoes that probably cost as much as her car.

"You outbid me."

Oh, so this was the woman who had just forced her to sell her grandma to the pimp down the street.

"I really wanted her. But you seemed to want her more."

So, she let Gia win? Why?

"Sorry," Gia said, not really meaning it.

"It's okay. I'm sure I'll find a way for you to make it up to me."

What the hell did *that* mean?

The unnamed woman walked away and disappeared into the crowd, and Gia went back into the main room.

After finding and following a server holding a tray of hors d'oeuvres, she put a couple of canapés on her napkin and ate as she looked around for her prize. She didn't see her for the rest of the night.

Gia went home in a cab, the envelope burning a hole in her purse.

Gia stared at the phone number in the letter from the auction. Snakes and butterflies fought a war inside her stomach as she tried to work up the nerve to call the woman she'd won.

A snake tied itself into a knot right in the pit of her stomach and settled there while she picked up the phone and dialed. She felt like throwing up. And stupid, calling a complete stranger to set up a date that was essentially being forced upon her. This woman would go out with her not because she wanted to, but because she was obligated to. What kind of fun would she have?

Gia began questioning the intelligence of this decision, this whole bidding thing.

On the other hand, what was to stop two strangers from having a good time together? It happened all the time. Who knew, maybe they would hit it off. No obligation, just fun.

What a disaster. She was about to hang up when she heard the dreaded word . . .

"Hello?"

"Uh . . . uh . . . H-hi. This is Gia. I won . . . I bid on . . . you know . . . the other night?"

"Oh, yeah. Hi." Was that amusement in her voice?

Gia had read in the letter that the woman's name was Jaylee Sinclair, which she hadn't heard during the auction because she was busy being swallowed up by the universe.

"So, you're calling to collect on the goods," Jaylee said.

Gia couldn't help but chuckle. "Yeah. Um, what's the usual thing?"

"Whatever you want it to be, I was told. I've never done this before." She paused, then asked, "Do you want to have dinner?"

Gia thought for a second and decided on another idea. "Well,

I have another one of these fundraiser things to go to, and I could use a date. Would you go with me? Or would that be, like, the most horrendous thing you could possibly think of?"

Jaylee chuckled. "No, not at all. You get to do with me whatever you like."

The sound of that suddenly made the sensations inside Gia's belly change considerably.

"Great. I'll pick you up."

Jaylee gave Gia her address, and with promises of a good time, she hung up.

A spark went up Gia's spine. She had the feeling that this date was going to be interesting. A sense of anticipation began to web itself throughout her nerves, a blooming expectation of something different, exciting . . . wild.

The fact that the event was only three days away was both a blessing and a curse. A blessing because she could go out with Jaylee before she lost her nerve, and a curse because it was too soon.

On the night of their date, she picked Jaylee up at her apartment and drove to the fundraiser. The conversation in the car was more comfortable than Gia had expected, and by the time they arrived at the venue, she felt as if she were on a real date with someone she knew. But as the valet took her key and they walked toward the front door, she reminded herself that this wasn't a real date. It was a pretend date. She felt like a whore. No, wait, she was the john. *Jesus Christ.*

Gia was uncomfortable at first. Could people see that her date had been purchased? Many of the guests had also been at the auction, so anyone who didn't know at the beginning of the evening was sure to know by the end.

Jaylee, however, was the epitome of cool. The looks they got didn't seem to bother her. A serene smile stayed on her face the entire evening, even as people asked questions. Jaylee answered them politely and maintained an even demeanor and that placid smile.

Jaylee was not only funny and charming, she had a raw sex appeal that seemed to rise from her body like an early morning mist off a river. Everyone around them felt it and turned their way as they walked around. Still, Jaylee remained cool.

Except, every once in a while, when they stopped to sip their cocktails, or when they had made a joke and laughed, Jaylee would turn her gaze on her, softly and sympathetically. But there was something else going on behind her eyes. Something raw and primal.

And it made Gia tremble.

The fundraiser was like any other such party: stuffy, boring, and fifty hours too long, populated by snooty rich people who could wipe their asses with hundred-dollar bills without blinking, and sound-tracked with live piano music that would put a coked-out rock band to sleep. The same obnoxious humor, the same sanctimonious blathering and cruel gossip veiled with insincere concern for the poor protagonist of whatever shocking story they were telling.

Jaylee must have sensed her boredom because she kept the conversation going and told jokes. After a while, she said, "Let's get out of here."

"Okay."

Jaylee took Gia by the hand and led her out of the building. Once outside, Gia reached into her purse for her valet ticket. While they waited for the car, Gia asked, "Where are we going?"

"To a party."

"This *is* a party."

"A different party. A friend of mine is having a thing. I told her I'd stop by if I could. Do you mind?"

Gia shook her head.

The valet brought her car around and after tipping him, Gia gave Jaylee the key. "Why don't you drive, since you know the way."

They drove in silence until they pulled up ten minutes later into the driveway of a private house.

They got out of the car, and Jaylee rang the bell. Sounds of music, laughter, and conversation emanated from the cracks of the door and the open windows. The door opened and a tall blonde smiled brightly. "Jaylee! You made it. I thought you were . . . occupied." She looked at Gia.

"Yeah, well, change of plans. This is Gia. Gia, this is Sue."

"Hi," Sue said, a wicked grin on her face. Her eyes flicked up and down Gia's body. Then she opened the door wider. "Come in. Get yourselves a drink at the bar and have a good time."

Jaylee led them to the bar, saying hello and kissing friends along the way, but not stopping to really talk.

The bar was a large antique hutch in the corner of the room, loaded with bottles of alcohol and a selection of glasses for different drinks. "What'll you have?" Jaylee asked.

"Whatever you're having," Gia replied.

Jaylee selected two martini glasses and picked up a shaker. After filling it with gin, dry vermouth, and cracked ice from an ice bucket, she fitted the top on and shook it vigorously. She removed the cap and poured the contents into the two glasses, and handed one to Gia.

"What, no olives?" Gia said, teasing, as she took hers.

"Why? You want something to eat?"

Gia's entire throat went dry. She just smiled and sipped her drink. It was so hot in there, and for some reason, it caused big lumps to form in her throat. It seemed improbable, but the next time she looked into her glass, it was empty.

"You wanna dance?" Jaylee asked.

"Sure." They put down their glasses and found a spot in the large living room, which was difficult, since the house was packed. Couples danced to mellow soul playing from the sound system. The crowd was mostly women, a few men, and even one or two straight couples, all well on their way to inebriation. Some were off to the sides making out, and one lesbian couple was making their way up the stairs.

Gia fell easily into Jaylee's arms, and Jaylee pulled her close. Just enough to drive her crazy. Gia's cocktail purse, which hung across her body, was a barrier so she pushed it to the side. The firm, tight muscles of Jaylee's body felt so good. Gia's flesh grew hot all over. And then they moved closer so that every curve of Gia's body fit into a groove of Jaylee's.

Jaylee pushed just a hair closer, probably not noticeable to anyone else, but for Gia, it was like worlds colliding. Her mouth was close to Gia's cheek, and Gia could feel her breath getting heavier and harder.

As they swayed, Jaylee ran her lips lightly along Gia's throat, making her shiver. Her shoulders, breasts, belly, and thighs all trembled with a deliciousness that made her want more.

The feel of Jaylee's tongue on the hollow of her throat, on her earlobe, and just behind her ear made her want to strip naked and let Jaylee do whatever she wanted. Right there in the living room. She didn't care.

Soft-looking and flushed red, Jaylee's lips were like magnets for Gia's. Gia was glad she'd worn a dress because she was sure that if she'd been wearing pants, a big wet spot would have shown up between her legs.

Their lips met in a hot, deep kiss that melted Gia to the core. Jaylee pulled away and looked up the stairs. She took Gia's hand and led her up, Gia offering no resistance, her underwear more soaked with each step.

At the top, Jaylee stopped in front of one door and opened it. They both peeked in to find that the bed was currently occupied by the couple she'd seen going up earlier, one's head buried in the other's pussy. Another bedroom was occupied as well, but there was one more door.

This room was empty and Jaylee grinned and pulled Gia inside. She shut the door and led Gia to the bed.

Gia didn't know who took off what or when, but it wasn't long before they were both naked and writhing against each other. Flames licked Gia's body with Jaylee's touch on every part of her, using hands, lips, and tongue.

Then Jaylee reached down the side of the bed and pulled something up.

"Where did that come from?" Gia asked, staring at the dildo in Jaylee's hand.

"Don't ask questions," Jaylee whispered.

Gia didn't. Her pussy ached, and she was beyond the point of no return, and it didn't really matter how that dildo came to be there. She also didn't know where the condom had come from, but Jaylee strapped on the dildo, rolled on the condom, and, with Gia's encouragement, moved quickly.

"Harder," Gia rasped. "*Harder*."

Jaylee put her weight into each thrust, her pelvis meeting Gia's in hard collisions, over and over. She pounded for several minutes, and then started to pull out slowly.

"What are you doing? Don't stop. Please," Gia croaked.

"Don't worry," Jaylee said, playfulness in her voice.

The door creaked open and Gia looked up. A redheaded woman walked in, and Gia thought she was hallucinating. It was the woman she'd outbid at the auction.

What the hell?

Jaylee leaned in close to Gia's ears. "Dina said she'd donate ten thousand dollars to the LGBT youth organization if we let her watch."

"What? You planned this? What the fuck?"

"No, I didn't. Not really. She just hoped things would work out this way."

"I'm not a freak show." Gia knew she hadn't said this with much conviction. She was on fire and needed to be sated.

"The auction was very important to me," Jaylee said, a sad note to her voice. "I used to be homeless. And Dina wants the money to go to HIV and STD screenings, birth control, stuff like that. It would do so much good."

Gia looked into her eyes a moment, then gave her consent by pulling Jaylee down on her for another hard, tongue-filled kiss. Jaylee pulled away and gave her a warm, grateful smile. She flashed a look at Dina, who sat in an upholstered chair a few feet away from the bed.

Jaylee moved herself out from between Gia's legs, and put one hand on her waist and the other on her thigh, nudging her. Gia realized what she wanted and rolled over. With her hands on Gia's hips, Jaylee pulled her up onto her knees.

The move to this position stoked Gia's urge, and now she felt like a fucking bomb. She bent her head to the mattress, tilted her ass up, and spread her legs as wide as she could. Her clit throbbed and she ached for Jaylee to fuck her until she exploded.

But Jaylee wasn't cooperating. Rather than reinserting the dildo, she toyed with her. Literally. She very gently rubbed the tip of the dildo up and down Gia's pussy, from just above her clit to her ass. Back and forth, up and down, making Gia insane. Whenever Gia pushed back, Jaylee pulled the dildo away, and every time she brought it close, Gia could feel the layer of moisture it pushed against. Rivulets of fluid trickled down her thighs, and she couldn't suppress the whimper that escaped her mouth.

She was dying, and Jaylee was taking way too much pleasure in torturing her.

Just when she thought she was going to have to make herself come, Jaylee put the tip of the dildo to her entrance and nudged, ever so slightly. Gia pushed back, but Jaylee just kept nudging it, just enough to make Gia homicidal.

"Please," Gia whispered hoarsely.

"I'm sorry. I can't hear you." Jaylee leaned over and cocked her head close to Gia's face, as if to hear her better.

"Please." Gia's voice was gurgled and strained. Her labored breathing made it difficult to speak.

"Please what?"

She could hear the smile in Jaylee's voice. That bitch. *Fucking bitch. Just fuck me!*

"Please fuck me," Gia managed to get out. Humiliation be damned. She really needed it *now*.

"Well, since you asked so nicely . . . "

Fucking bitch.

After what was an agonizing, tortuous eternity, Jaylee slipped the dildo into Gia's pussy, so smoothly. No resistance, no pressure. Gia gasped and tilted her ass up even more. Jaylee pumped slowly at first, but Gia pushed back and forth repeatedly, so Jaylee pumped harder and faster.

Gia swam in waves of pleasure as Jaylee fucked her tirelessly. But after a while, Gia's back began to twinge. So she pushed herself up onto only her knees, and leaned into Jaylee.

Jaylee welcomed her against her own body with an arm around Gia's waist. Gia rode the dildo while Jaylee squeezed and fondled her breasts. Feeling Jaylee's breasts pressed against her back was sublime, and she suddenly wanted to come just so she could throw Jaylee down, rip off the dildo, and suck her pussy.

Then she noticed Dina in the chair. She'd forgotten about her, but now she was hard to miss. Dina had lifted her skirt and had her hand down her underwear. To Gia's surprise, she was turned on even more.

Hot breath warmed the skin on her neck as Jaylee nibbled on her. Jaylee ran her tongue along Gia's neck from her collarbone to her ear. Every nerve ending in Gia's body sparked, electrified, and she shuddered. She reached behind and slipped a finger into the gap between the strap-on belt and Jaylee's crotch. The wetness she felt there was exquisite.

She pulled her hand away when Jaylee reached in front of her and began massaging her clit with one hand, while squeezing her breast with the other, pinching and pulling the nipple. She bit Gia's neck and stroked until the pressure in Gia's pussy became unbearable. Somewhere deep inside her, a volcano erupted, starting as a rumble and increasing in strength, bubbling up, shooting through her, until it exploded. Gia came so hard, she needed Jaylee to hold her up, which she kindly did. Hot lava coated Gia's thighs and her pussy pulsed around the dildo.

Gia trembled and convulsed for some time, until the volcano was empty. Jaylee's lips remained on her jaw, an unexpectedly tender gesture.

But what she didn't expect were the sounds coming from behind her as Jaylee pumped slightly, but obviously in a way that made the dildo rub against her own clit. Gripping Gia's hips, she came, groaning. This was complemented by the moans of orgasm coming from Dina, her hand moving inside her underwear until she grew calm.

When Jaylee was done, Gia dropped down onto her elbows and slowly pulled forward, allowing the dildo to slide out gradually. When the head slipped out, she gasped and fell onto the bed, Jaylee collapsing beside her.

Gia looked at Dina, who got up, fixed her skirt, and smiled at them before walking out and closing the door quietly.

"I really wanted to make you come," Gia said, disappointed.

"You did make me come."

"I mean, I wanted to eat you."

"You still can."

"Can you go again?"

"Mm, maybe not tonight. But maybe another night," Jaylee said, sounding hopeful.

Gia looked at Jaylee, her features flushed and relaxed, and wondered if things would've gone this far if she hadn't been so hormonal. She decided that maybe this was nature's way of repaying women for all those years of bleeding, pain, and inconvenience—by letting them have a fucking good time when all was said and done.

"Yeah," Gia said. "Definitely another night."

Jaylee got up, removed the strap-on, and took it to the bathroom. Gia heard the water running for a moment, then Jaylee came out. Gia didn't know what she had done with the dildo, but things had apparently been prearranged.

"How about tomorrow?" Jaylee smiled, wicked yet sincere, picking up their conversation.

Gia nodded and smiled, and after they had dressed, she followed Jaylee back to the party, glad she'd put in that bid.

RAINBOW'S END

Emily L. Byrne

Lizzie got off the bus and stared warily down the dark, empty street ahead of her. It figured that someone would stick a queer bookstore called Rainbow's End at the ass-end of town, out past the one surviving queer bar or anything else that might pull people in. If she squinted, she could see a rainbow flag flapping in the breeze over a storefront about two blocks away. Now she just had to get there.

Right. She took a deep breath. This was part of why she'd moved to the big bad city, after all: the hope of finding other people like her. She could handle dark streets in a scary part of town. Her cold fingers closed around the small bottle of pepper spray in her jacket pocket for reassurance while she told herself it wasn't that bad, she wasn't that freaked out.

She looked around at the quiet bar across the street. There was a late-night diner down a few blocks. There were houses and apartment buildings on the side streets. Just like real people lived here. She was just overreacting, letting her small-town background get the best of her. Lizzie's fingers crossed over the small bottle in her pocket as she took a few steps away from the well-lit bus stop.

A sound behind her made her jump as an androgynous-looking couple crossed the street and stepped onto the corner behind her. Between their battered leather jackets, boots, and buzzed hair, Lizzie recognized her people. At least, she hoped they were her people. They were laughing as they brushed past her to walk toward that tiny rainbow flag in the distance, Doc Martins thudding against the concrete.

Lizzie stared after them, wondering what to do next. They must have seen her black lace skirt and leggings, her witchy jacket, her clunky heels and black-rimmed eyes, and dismissed her as a straight girl. Maybe. Or maybe they hadn't seen her at all.

Well, they were going to notice her now. Lizzie narrowed her brown eyes, yanked her tattered leather jacket tighter around her ample curves, and took off after them. "Hey! You going to the reading? Can I walk with you?"

They paused and glanced at each other. Then the tall blonde gave her a crooked grin that gave her goose bumps. "Sure. Probably should have asked. Not too many mundane folks up this end of the row after dark unless they live around here. We just got distracted. You a friend of Alyssa's?"

"Mundane? Like, boring?" Lizzie had to tilt her head back to look either of them in the eye, heels or no heels. She bit back a sigh as they all started walking again and she had to scramble to get caught up. "No, I don't know Alyssa. I just like her stories and the stuff she posts online. I was really excited to see that she was coming here." She sounded like a total fan girl, but then that crooked grin was still making the butterflies dance in her stomach.

"Mundane like . . . not like us, whatever we may be or call ourselves," the shorter, dark-haired one said. "I'm Sam Vargas.

This is A.J. Williams. They, them," they pointed to themselves. "She or her," Sam added, pointing to A.J.

Lizzie tried not to look startled or freaked out; no one back home ever even asked about stuff like pronouns, just assumed. But when she thought about it, it was kind of cool. Made it easier to understand where people were coming from. "Oh. Cool. I'm Lizzie and I'm she and her, I guess." Lizzie looked up to realize that the bookstore, all bravely lit up against the night and flying its rainbow flag, was only a few yards ahead of them.

A screeching noise behind them made them all whip around as a carload of guys shot past, screaming, "Dykes! Fags!" One of them threw something and Lizzie instinctively ducked and raced for the nearest shelter. A bottle smashed on the sidewalk near them, showering them with glass and Sam screamed curses after the car, shaking their fists. The bookstore suddenly disgorged a bunch of women and queer folks, several with phones in their hands.

And Lizzie looked up to find out that she had somehow . . . tucked herself into A.J.'s arms. She turned beet-red and stumbled back. "I'm so sorry. I didn't even realize I was . . . I did . . . " She trailed off and A.J. reached out and carefully squeezed her shoulder.

"No worries. The fuckers scared me too."

Then they were surrounded by the crowd and herded into the bookshop. For a couple of minutes, Lizzie was too overwhelmed by all the voices and faces to even look around. "I got the license plate!" someone shouted gleefully.

"Is everyone okay? No cuts or anything?" someone else behind the counter yelled.

"Where are the folks who were outside when those fools drove by?" This from someone at the front of the room.

Sam tugged A.J. and Lizzie forward. "That would be us. I don't think any of us got cut, just freaked out." They gave a tense look at Lizzie and A.J. for confirmation, then relaxed a little at their nods.

"Oh man, what a bunch of assholes! I'm Alyssa and I know Sam and A.J., but I haven't met you before." Lizzie found her hand being gently shaken by a goth vision: pierced lips, black eyeliner, black lace, platform boots, and the bluest eyes she'd ever seen. From a billion miles away, she heard A.J. tell this gorgeous creature her name.

Then the room spun around and her knees gave out. A.J. caught her before she hit the grimy carpet and half-carried her over to a big overstuffed couch. Someone else handed her a glass of water and steadied it in her trembling hands while she drank. She closed her eyes, leaned back, and took a couple of deep breaths. When she opened them and blinked against the harsh ceiling lights, there was a circle of anxious faces peering down at her.

"I'm okay. I think. Nothing like this has ever—I mean, I . . . " she trailed off, conscious of Alyssa standing over her and A.J.'s muscular frame just next to her. The butterflies in her stomach were back, this time whirling up to choke her words back. She took another drink from the glass. "Thank you," she murmured at A.J., embarrassment making her blush even harder.

What was she supposed to do now? Was there some kind of etiquette for getting harassed by asshole guys, then getting rescued by a store full of hot women and other folks? She shivered a little, then took another drink. A.J.'s leg brushed hers and it sent a warm flush through her. It felt like all the adrenaline of the last thirty minutes was starting to settle in her pussy and she squirmed against the couch, trying to ease the growing ache without being too obvious.

Everything around the couch was a whirl of conversations and introductions. A few moments later, she remembered meeting the owners of the store and a bunch of Alyssa's friends and one of Sam's partners and after that, she lost track of who was connected to whom. Throughout it all, A.J. stayed put and she found herself nestling closer, letting A.J.'s warmth wash over her.

Then Alyssa went up to the podium and started reading, passionate words rolling out of her mouth to fill the small store. Her voice caressed their ears, her words like tongues on Lizzie's skin. Despite her fears and her anxiety, she couldn't help but respond. The stories were angry, erotic, fierce, and Alyssa read each short piece perfectly. The room erupted into cheers each time she paused to drink from her water bottle.

She paused to answer a question and in that moment, Lizzie was conscious of being pressed up against A.J., of Sam on the other side of her, of Alyssa's words licking their way up her thighs and every inch of her exposed skin. A.J. gave her a crooked grin and a slow onceover that made Lizzie flush before she grinned back.

It was warm in the store, warmer on the crowded couch, and Lizzie wanted . . . wanted so much. Wanted A.J.'s long fingers between her legs, wanted Alyssa's nipples in her mouth, wanted . . . all of them. Every last woman and genderqueer and nonbinary person in the store. All of them. Tits, pussies, asses, any erogenous zones they wanted to share. Lizzie shivered at the idea. She'd never felt like this before. Was it just her? She was afraid to look around, afraid to wonder.

But that fear didn't last long. A.J. nudged her shoulder, making her look up from the floor. "You doing okay?"

Lizzie fell into A.J.'s blue eyes. "Umm . . . yeah. I think so. Alyssa is really, really good." She hesitated for a minute, then added, "I'm so glad that I made it here tonight. Even with those assholes and their fucking beer bottle."

"Us too." Sam nudged her shoulder from the other side, grinned at both of them, then turned away and kissed their date.

Lizzie looked away, aroused and embarrassed. A.J. caught her mood, like she was reading her mind, or so it felt to Lizzie. "Hey, I could use some air, but I think I'd like to pass on going out front for the time being. Misha and Lou have a little yard out back. You want to step outside with me for a couple of minutes?" A.J.'s voice was a quiet purr against her ear and Lizzie could feel herself blush.

Part of Lizzie hesitated. She hardly knew this woman or her friends or anyone in the store. And she'd only ever kissed another girl once. What if she screwed up something, anything, and they all made fun of her and kicked her out? Maybe she wasn't really that into girls. Maybe . . . she popped up from the couch before she could lose her nerve. "Yes! Let's go."

Lizzie thought she heard a giggle or two behind them, but she didn't turn around. Instead, she marched straight for the back of the store, then realized that she had no idea where this patio was. She paused and stared fiercely at a bookcase, like there was a title that caught her attention. And it probably had, or would have, under other circumstances. One that didn't include a hot woman leaning over her shoulder.

A.J. looked at the shelf in front of them. "Seems a bit theoretical. I'm a praxis kind of gal, myself. How about you, Lizzie?" She chuckled quietly in Lizzie's ear, sending hot waves up and down her body.

"Where's this patio of yours?" Lizzie glanced around. Someone else was stepping up to the mike, sheaf of pages in hand. "Looks like the open mike is going to start." The store looked different from this angle, a little darker, more chaotic, the crowd a sea of shaved heads and dyed hair. Nothing like back home. "I love this." She grinned up at A.J.

"Me too. You write?"

Lizzie blushed. Was she that obvious? A.J. opened a door and ushered her outside. "A little. But not like anything I could read here or get published or anything."

"Yeah? I think it's cool that you write. What kind of stuff?"

They were outside now, standing under the stars on an uneven brick patio with a bunch of garage-sale chairs and small tables scattered around it. A couple of recycled barrels full of flowers and vegetables and some metal and wooden artwork completed the picture. They were also alone for the first time. Lizzie looked at A.J., looked at how close she was standing, and blurted out, "I'd really like to kiss you right now."

A.J.'s smile lit up her long face for a moment. "I think we can make that happen." Her arms wrapped around Lizzie slowly, carefully, like she was afraid of scaring her off. Then Lizzie's arms were around A.J.'s neck and they were awkwardly figuring out where everyone's nose should go. Once their lips met, Lizzie was very, very sure that she liked girls and liked this one quite a bit right now.

Things got a bit blurry after that. A.J. tasted like pop and salsa and breath mints and Lizzie had a moment of pure self-consciousness wondering if she tasted like her dinner and if that was gross. Then she lost herself exploring A.J.'s mouth with her tongue and reveling in her own mouth being explored in turn. She pulled them closer together as A.J.'s hands slipped lower, then wandered over to her jacket's zipper.

The autumn night was chilly enough that Lizzie shivered a little when A.J. unzipped her jacket, in spite of all the heat they were generating. A.J. unzipped her own jacket and used it to wrap around both them to pull Lizzie even closer. Lizzie's black lace top did little to conceal her hardened nipples and she moaned into A.J.'s mouth when the other woman's thumb grazed first one, then the other. A.J. sat down on one of the sturdier tables and pulled Lizzie into her lap without breaking off their kiss.

From somewhere nearby, Lizzie heard the patio door open, heard voices, then heard the door shut again, this time closing out the sound of several people laughing. She flushed and pulled away, but didn't release her arms from A.J.'s neck. A.J. laughed. "No worries. It's not the first time." Lizzie's jaw dropped. "No! I don't mean me, I just mean, you know, in general." A.J.'s blush showed up splendidly despite the dim lights on the patio.

Lizzie paused before she started laughing, mostly at herself and their situation. This was nuts. Who was she to be jealous or surprised about anything this almost complete stranger had done before they met? "I'm kinda . . . new to all this." She gestured around, in a way that suggested she could mean a whole bunch of things.

"And this is moving too fast. We've already had a rough night." A.J. looked adorably contrite in the shadowy light.

"Wait, what? No." Lizzie stumbled over her words in her hurry to get this very cute, hot woman to reconsider. They might not have ever met tonight, they could have been killed by those assholes in the car, A.J. could have had a girlfriend or partner waiting for her in the store, a thousand possibilities could have stood between them and this moment—but none of those things had happened. This was her big chance, dammit, and she wasn't going to waste it. "I want this. A lot."

She plastered herself to A.J.'s torso, her thighs on either side of the other's legs, and kissed her as hard as she could. A.J. stiffened, then relaxed into the kiss. She pulled Lizzie down so that she straddled her lap and Lizzie gasped as A.J. broke the kiss off to run her tongue down the exposed skin of Lizzie's neck. "Me too." A.J.'s response was muffled, but enthusiastic.

A.J. slipped one arm around her waist and tucked the other around Lizzie's ass, rocking her hips so their crotches touched. Lizzie reached down between them and gave A.J. a tentative rub through her jeans and A.J. gave her neck a pleased groan and a gentle nip in response. A.J.'s free hand was up Lizzie's skirt now, stroking her thigh under her tights and sending a spark through her with every touch.

Lizzie felt A.J. fumbling with the top button on her lace top and reached up to undo it herself. She leaned in to run her tongue along the edge of A.J.'s ear, drinking in her scent and the taste of her skin. One button slipped open, then the next, and A.J. buried her face between Lizzie's large breasts with a happy sigh. Lizzie's skin burned at the touch of A.J.'s hot mouth exploring her skin. They wrapped each other closer, merging together into a tangle of limbs and mouths and heat and desire, enough to drive off the chilly air.

A.J. shifted Lizzie over so that she straddled one of A.J.'s thighs and Lizzie moved so that her knee was between A.J.'s legs. She undid another button on her top and groaned deep in her throat as A.J. pulled one of her hardened nipples into her mouth. Her hands felt clumsy but it didn't stop her from scrambling over every bit of A.J. that she could reach under her jacket. Touching, stroking, pinching—she wanted them to be naked, wanted their hot flesh to fuse together into a naked wet pile of need and fulfillment.

She pushed her knee harder into A.J.'s crotch and was rewarded with a quiet groan as the other woman's hips rocked forward, driving against her pressure. Lizzie wasn't sure what to do next, but A.J. seemed to know what would work for her. She rubbed herself faster against Lizzie's leg, moaning softly into her breasts as her grip tightened. Finally, just when Lizzie thought she might burst from lack of air and the suspense of wondering what might happen next, A.J. came with a groan, her whole body shaking under and around Lizzie's, her head thrown back as she gasped for air.

When she stopped quivering and opened her eyes, Lizzie grinned down at her and kissed her hard. "That was so hot," she murmured when they came up for air. "I've never met anyone like you before," she added truthfully, then bit off everything else she had planned to follow that up with. Maybe this was a one-time thing. Maybe A.J. did this every week. Maybe . . .

A.J. pulled her forward, like she was thinking that she could make Lizzie come with the pressure from her leg alone. And it just might happen. Lizzie was tingly with arousal and excitement. She ached so badly that she wasn't sure it would ever go away. Yet, with all that, she couldn't relax enough to come this way.

It only took a few minutes for A.J. to catch on, without her even saying anything. She gently pushed Lizzie backward, stood up, and changed their positions. A moment later, she was kneeling between Lizzie's legs, running her hand up the inside of her thigh. "Do you like these tights?" Her voice was gravelly with desire and the look in her blue eyes made Lizzie shiver all over.

"N-no. Want me to take them off?" Lizzie thought that right now she might be willing to sacrifice an internal organ that she wasn't using, anything to get A.J.'s hands and mouth back on her body.

"I think I've got a better solution." A.J.'s breathy laugh warmed Lizzie's thighs and she could feel fingers against her thighs and crotch. Then, just as she reined in the impulse to hump A.J.'s hands, there was a small metallic click followed by a blast of cold air on her suddenly bare skin. "Just opening up an easy access panel." A.J. laughed again, then lowered her mouth to Lizzie's bare skin.

Lizzie nearly levitated off the table. A.J.'s fingers were on her panties, then inside them, then inside her. A.J.'s mouth was hot and wet against the cotton covering her clit. Lizzie wrapped her fingers in what she could grasp of A.J.'s short-cropped hair, trying to pull her closer, trying to ride her tongue and fingers to an elusive release. She gasped for air as A.J. rubbed her thumb against her clit, sending shock waves through her.

Her clit burned from the unaccustomed pressure while her nerve endings vibrated with every new touch, every new smell. She lost herself in a fantasy of naked skin and silky sheets, of A.J. thrusting into her, sucking her clit, tasting and savoring her until she couldn't hold back anymore. She saw sparks until she convulsed with a yell that made her clap her hand over her mouth as soon as she recovered some measure of self-control.

She could feel her face go bright red as A.J. grinned up from between her thighs. "Well, if they had any questions inside about what we were up to, they don't anymore." She stroked Lizzie's quivering skin for a few more moments, letting her ride out the aftershocks. She stood up and looked at Lizzie, who stared back at her in a roiling mix of horror and lust. "It's okay. It's not like . . . wait, was this your first time?" Lizzie responded with a stunned nod. "Oh wow, I wish I'd known. I could have taken you . . . well, no. Who am I kidding? I wanted you now and this was really hot." A.J. leaned in and kissed her gently, then began buttoning up her shirt.

"Is everyone going to make fun of us? Was I really that loud?" Lizzie hunched miserably as she clambered slowly off the table.

"Wait, wait. No, hon. They'll tease us a little, sure, but this isn't like high school or something. The mean girls aren't going to shun us from their lunchroom table. If anything, they'll be jealous that they weren't out here having fun." A.J. zipped up her jacket and gave her a long hug. "And Alyssa will be flattered that she inspired an orgasm or two. She says that's the best tribute her work can receive." A.J. laughed again, quiet and sexy in the cool air.

Lizzie drew in a deep breath and realized that she was cold, much colder than she would have expected, given what they'd been doing. A quick glance around showed her that the only exit from the patio was through the store, so there was no avoiding the crowd inside. Besides, if she bolted, who knew when she'd see A.J. again? "Okay," she began hesitantly, gathering up a little more courage. "Could we maybe go out for coffee after this?"

"As opposed to humping each other on the bus? You bet. You ready to go back inside? I'm getting pretty cold." A.J. reached out and took Lizzie's hand in hers and waited for her nod. Then together, they stepped back into the store, filled with light and laughter and words that lit up the night like magic.

OLIVER: TWISTED

Nanisi Barrett D'Arnuk

I looked out across the field of people and shook my head. All these women, and not one could look at me. Not that they knew I was there, but just once I wished that someone would look up and see me, or at least look like they saw me. That's all I wanted: just one woman. But, like every other night, not one raised her eyes. *Just once*, I thought, *at least one*.

I watched the women focus on their cards, not letting a thought that someone was watching disturb their concentration. The dealers dealt and shuffled, then dealt and shuffled, and dealt and shuffled. The players won and lost without looking around, without a second thought for the bubbles in the ceiling that contained surveillance cameras.

This is an easy and boring job, except on those rare nights when someone, either too drunk or wanting more money, tries something foolish. Then we get to watch interesting things, like someone being surreptitiously thrown out of the casino; hidden, so the other patrons won't be disturbed. Tonight I watched the cutie in the second seat at the blackjack table. She had short dark hair that looked great from the top. So did her voluptuous cleavage that showed when she leaned back. These were the ones that made this job interesting. I could be a voyeur without the fear of being discovered or guilt that I was staring.

Look up, look up I thought, trying to concentrate hard enough that my thoughts would get through to the woman. But she didn't look up. She simply played her cards, the pile of chips in front of her rising and falling as the evening wore on. *Come on, cutie, concentrate,* I projected. *Look up at the ceiling.*

My name is Cheryl Oliver and I've worked here over two years, viewing the monitors to make sure nothing gets out of hand down on the casino floor. It isn't a hard job, the hours are great and the pay passable. It's easier than any other place I've worked and at least I don't have to communicate with customers with such inane lines as "Do you want fries with that?" or "Thank you. Drive through."

I work the late shift, six p.m. to two a.m. That gives me afternoons to run errands or do whatever needs to be done. I work Saturday evening to Thursday morning. That's the good part; I have Thursday evening, all day Friday and Saturdays until six free.

"Hey, Oliver, ready for a break?" came a voice over my headset.

"Yeah, Bruce. Thanks," I answered.

"Logan's on her way up."

"Going on a break," I signaled to Jimmy, who sat at the station next to mine. He gave me a thumbs-up. That's what communication is like all the time here. There are weeks when I don't hear another human voice at all, except for Bruce or Darren, the night managers.

In a couple of minutes I heard footsteps on the stairs. I stood, took my headphones off, and stretched to get the kinks out of my back.

"Hey, Cher, how's it going tonight?" Jane Logan asked. She

walked into the room and threw her backpack on the floor beside the chair.

"Pretty quiet tonight. Not much happening."

"Any cute ones down there?" Jane asked, scanning the row of monitors.

"Check out the cleavage in seat two at blackjack table three."

Janie looked and let out a low whistle. "Nice," she whispered. "Very nice."

"She's probably straight," I reminded her.

"Just window shopping."

I had to chuckle as I picked up my backpack and headed for the stairs.

"I'll be back in twenty."

"Take your time," Janie called after me.

I went down the stairs and walked slowly across the casino floor, holding a glass of soda one of the waitresses had handed me. The bartenders knew we'd need one as soon as we appeared. I looked up at the bubble and gave a cheerful wave. I wasn't sure who was watching, but it was nice to be recognized once in a while.

The casino was loud and the clientele boisterous. Everyone was happy that it was the weekend and those that weren't winning were sitting in the bar having a glass of liquid *that's-okay* or at least a bottle of *poor-baby* with their buddies. Others were sitting at the tables having the $4.99 special: a six-ounce sirloin, a small baked potato, and a salad.

I walked all around the casino, watching people play blackjack, roulette, or half a dozen other table games. The woman I'd seen at the blackjack table wasn't there. Maybe she'd gone home, but at eleven o'clock on a Saturday night? Maybe I hadn't recognized her. I hadn't actually looked at her face.

I cruised by the slot machines but there were so many rows of them, I didn't get to see them all. Besides, there's not a lot of room between the rows so it was hard to get through without bumping into everyone. The band in the bar was taking a break so there was nothing to watch there, either. Slow night.

Then I walked into the ladies' room. As I was washing my hands, a woman came out of one of the stalls.

"Hi," she greeted me.

"Hello." I reached for a paper towel.

"You look like you work here." She pressed the soap nozzle as she ogled my gray shirt and slacks.

"Upstairs," I responded. Then I took a good look at the woman. I could have been wrong but this was the cleavage on seat two of blackjack table three. She was shorter than I'd expected; maybe two inches shorter than me.

"Do they really watch us from up there?"

I nodded, not trusting my voice not to crack.

"Is that what you do?" the woman asked, as she rinsed her hands and reached for a paper towel.

"Yes. We're always watching."

She held out her hand and introduced herself. "Jerri Anderson."

"Cheryl Oliver." I finished wiping my hands and shook hers. "I haven't seen you in here before."

When Jerri raised her eyebrows, I clarified, "Not in the ladies' room, I mean in the casino."

Jerri chuckled. "I'm visiting with my sister. She's playing slots."

I could only nod.

"Does everyone wear uniforms up there?" She reached out and straightened my collar and necktie.

"Most, not everyone."

"Do you wear it at home, too?"

"Not usually." I chuckled. "Just when I'm on duty."

"Then I'd like to see if you look as nice when you're not wearing a uniform."

I swallowed. If I hadn't known better, I'd have sworn that this woman was coming on to me.

"I usually change before I go home."

"What time is that?" Jerri asked.

"I get off at two."

"Ah. Do you have time for a cup of coffee right now? I doubt you can drink on duty."

I took a deep breath. "I'm sorry, I can't. But if you're still around when I get off, I'll have one with you then." If she was going to come on to me, I was going to return the favor.

"I'll look for you, then." With that, Jerri smiled, winked, and left the ladies' room.

I took a deep breath and let it out slowly. *Wow! did that really just happen?* I threw the paper towel into the trash and headed for the monitor room.

"Anything I should watch for?" I asked Janie when I got back upstairs.

"Nah. Pretty quiet tonight. I lost track of your cleavage, though," Janie told me.

"I ran into her in the ladies' room," I had to admit.

Janie looked at me, her eyes wide. "And?"

I shrugged. "Her name's Jerri and she's here with her sister."

"And?" Janie pushed for more.

I looked down at the table in front of the monitors and straightened the pads of papers there. "She liked my uniform," I said without looking up.

Janie laughed. "Is she straight?"

"I have no idea," I shrugged with a small frown.

"You're losing your edge, girl. You used to be able to pick them out right away."

I laughed. "The cleavage looks better up close."

"How close?" Janie asked as she picked up her backpack.

"Close enough."

Janie laughed as she walked over to Jimmy. "Break time, buddy," she told him as she slid into the chair he vacated.

I also slid into my chair.

"Well, look at that!" Janie called out to me.

I looked into the monitors. Jerri was back at a blackjack table and was waving to us.

"You must have made a good impression." Janie laughed.

I licked my lips. Should I tell Janie that Jerri was going to meet me after my shift was over? *No, better not,* I thought. *I don't know what to expect.*

When Jimmy came back from break, Janie spelled Blake and then Willy, who were watching the slot machines. Then she got ready to leave.

"Your friend seems to be waiting for something. Did you make a date with her?" she asked me. "That must be her sister over on the second rank of slots. She keeps going over to talk to her."

"She's over by the roulette wheel now." I didn't dare answer Janie's question.

"Well, good luck," Janie whispered. "Don't forget to tell me what happens."

"You'll be the first to know," I assured her.

At 2:00 a.m., the next shift arrived. Jimmy, Blake, Willy, and I got ready to leave. I first went into the ladies' room and changed my shirt, then went out onto the casino floor.

"I like you better in uniform," I heard.

I whipped around. Jerri was behind me.

"Hi," I greeted her. "I didn't know if you'd still be here."

"I told you I would."

I grinned, a little embarrassed. "Are you ready for that cup of coffee?"

"You still want coffee? Aren't you hungry?" Jerri asked.

"I usually go home and make myself something."

"We can do that," Jerri stated. "Do you have a car?"

I nodded.

"I'll tell my sister she can leave without me."

Before I could respond, Jerri had walked away.

"You'll get her home?" Jerri's sister walked with us to the lobby. Jerry and her sister were both about the same size with dark hair, although the sister's was quite a bit longer.

"I'll be fine, sis," Jerri said before I could respond.

"All right. Should I expect you anytime soon?"

Jerri looked at me. "I'll call," she told her sister.

The sister looked at me. "Be careful," she said.

Jerri laughed as if it were the funniest thing she'd heard. "I'll take care of her," she said.

Sister gave me a strange look, but I couldn't tell what she was thinking. She rolled her eyes.

Jerri and her sister kissed good-bye, and then Jerri turned back to me.

"Do you live near here?" she asked.

"Just about fifteen minutes at this time of night," I told her.

"Then, let's go." She smiled.

I felt light-headed as she looked up at me. I pulled my keys out of my pocket so I wouldn't stare into her eyes. Taking a deep breath, I said, "All right. I'm back there." I pointed to the employee parking lot.

I drive an old pickup truck. It has a bench seat, not bucket seats, and Jerri slid closer to me than was necessary.

"I saw you wave up at us," I told her, for lack of anything better to say.

"Did you enjoy it?"

I may have blushed. "Yes," I told her. "Very few people even acknowledge that we're there."

"No, did *you* enjoy it?" she pushed on.

"Yeah, I did," I admitted.

"Good." She leaned over and kissed my cheek.

To cover my embarrassment, I asked, "Do you live near here?"

"About a hundred miles away. Just outside Wichita. But I get down here to visit my sister two, maybe three times a year . . . unless I have a better reason."

"What would be a better reason?"

Jerry smiled. "Someone more exciting than my sister."

The rest of the drive, Jerri asked me about my job and explained hers.

When we got to my apartment complex, I pulled my truck into my assigned space.

"Well, we're here," I said. *Now, why did I say that? Of course we're here.*

We got out of the truck and walked to my door. I slipped my key into the lock and held the door open for her.

"This is a sweet little apartment," she said, looking around the living room. "What are the neighbors like?"

"I have no idea," I said, and closed and locked the door. "They're already asleep when I get home and they're just coming home from work when I leave. I have most of the day to myself. There aren't many kids in this complex."

"So you don't know your neighbors?"

"I see them around but I can't say I know them. I can recognize a few faces but I don't know any names. I imagine I'm just that chick that lives in unit twenty-four."

"How did you luck into this place? My sister knows all her neighbors. She can't make a move without everyone knowing about it."

"I think working nights might have something to do with it. I saw a for-rent sign on the corner. The rest simply fell in place." I went over to the refrigerator, opened it, and bent down to look inside. "What do you want to eat?" I asked, looking into it.

"You."

That stopped me. I'd never met anyone quite that . . . that . . . blatant. I turned as I heard her laugh.

"Didn't expect that, did you?" she asked as I stood staring at her.

"Well . . . no.

"Let me guess," she continued, "you're usually the one to make the first move." She chuckled at me.

I took a deep breath. "Mostly." It seemed I'd been taking a lot of deep breaths tonight.

"Then this must be new to you." It looked like she was enjoying my discomfort. "Maybe we'll have to see what else is new to you."

With that, she stepped forward and started to unbutton my shirt. I didn't stop her.

As she undid the front clasp of my bra she asked, "Where do you want to do this?"

"Do this?" I asked in my totally dazed way.

"You do want to make love with me, don't you? Or have I totally misread you?"

I could feel the heat rising on my face and in my crotch. How could I respond to that?

"The bedroom's over there," I answered, pointing down the hall.

"That will work," she said as she headed for it.

I closed the refrigerator door and followed. When I got into the bedroom, Jerri was looking through the rack of neckties that hung from the closet doorknob.

"Do you wear all of these?" She let the ties flow through her fingers.

"Not all at once," I said.

She laughed loudly. "I didn't think so."

"These black ones are part of my uniform; the rest are fun."

She smiled up at me. "There are quite a few black ones."

I think I blushed. "Well . . . " I said, a little embarrassed, "I spill food a lot and it always ends up on my tie, so I have to make sure there's always a clean one."

She laughed the cutest light laugh. Then she slipped my shirt back over my shoulders.

I drew her into my arms and kissed her. Oh god! What a wonderful kiss!

I continued kissing her, only stopping long enough to lift her shirt over her head. We couldn't get each other's clothes off fast enough.

I pulled her down onto the bed with me. We still hadn't stopped kissing. I looked down at her. She was perfect. Not muscular, but not soft, either.

Her skin against mine was amazing. And her breasts! They were full and firm and fit into my hands so perfectly.

What was I doing? This was a woman I knew nothing about, except that she lived near Wichita, Kansas, and had great tits. But this kissing thing was going to my head.

Then she rolled over on top of me, and kissed my breasts.

"Wait just a minute," she whispered and got off the bed. When she returned, she had the rack of ties.

"What are those for?" I asked.

"Wait and see." She winked, and straddled me.

She made a slipknot in one of them, then placed it around my left wrist. I could only stare at her. I was shocked by what she was doing. She tied the tie to the brass bedpost.

Then she started a slipknot in another.

"Whoa, whoa, wait a minute," I said, and reached to untie the first one.

"No." She laughed as she grabbed my right hand. "You'll rip it."

I must have been wide-eyed. I wasn't sure what was happening. Well . . . I knew, but I wasn't sure I wanted to believe it. I'd heard about stuff like this but I'd never experienced it. Not that I wanted to. Before I could protest again, she had my right arm tied to the other bedpost.

"Uh . . . " I started. What was this? I hadn't told anyone I was taking her home and her sister didn't know who I was or where I lived.

"Shh," she whispered, covering my mouth with her lips. "Just wait and see. Or not, as the case might be." With that, she took a third tie and looped it around my head, covering my eyes.

"Jerri," I began, but before I could say anything else, I felt her lips around my nipple. I inhaled sharply.

"Isn't this better?" I heard her say. "When you can't see something, it makes the feel of it even more amazing."

"I can't do this, Jerri," I protested.

"Sure you can. Just give me five minutes, then if you really can't, say *Jerri from Wichita* and I'll stop. Just five minutes? Please?"

Well . . . I thought. *Should I?*

She didn't wait. "Are you ticklish?"

"A little," I answered

"Good."

Then I felt her fingers traveling ever so lightly down my body. I tried to move, but she was wedged between my legs. Every time I bent my knee to get a little leverage, she'd pull my ankle to lower my leg again.

"Am I going to have to tie your legs down, too?" she asked.

"I'm not used to this," I told her. I could feel nervous laughter threatening to erupt out of me. "I've never done this before."

"Then you're going to have to trust me, aren't you?" She took my other nipple in her mouth while her hands roamed my body.

It was incredible. I don't think I'd ever been turned on so much in my life. This had to be a big leap of faith.

I could feel my body getting hotter and hotter. Even her little bites were driving me crazy. She'd been right; each touch was magnified thousands of times. I didn't know where she'd be next. Soon, I thought I'd go out of my mind. I wanted to hold her, to kiss her, to make love to *her*, too. I wasn't used to lovemaking that was all one-sided.

"All right," she said, "that's five minutes. Should I continue or go home?"

No, I didn't want her to go home.

"Continue?" I whispered.

Her hand found my crotch. I inhaled, trying to keep from screaming.

"Are these walls thick?" she asked.

"I have no idea," was my answer and at that point, I didn't care.

"Maybe we'll have to find out." She took my clit between her fingers and rubbed it. But she didn't *just* rub it. No, first she was on one side and then the other. Before I knew what was happening, the sensations were building up. I was moaning and gasping. I couldn't control myself. She was everywhere. I was nowhere. I had no grasp on reality. There was nothing past the bed. There was no bed. There was just that incredible feeling blossoming inside of me.

I came to the edge of orgasm several times, but she knew immediately how to slow me down before I fell over that edge. Over and over again I teetered on the brink, but she always pulled me back. I was starting to lose it. I wasn't sure how much longer I could take this.

"You ready?" I heard her say. I think I nodded. Then the volcano erupted.

"Jerri!" I screamed. I don't know how that name found its way into my mouth. "Good god, I can't . . . no . . . how . . . ?" I couldn't put together a cohesive sentence.

But she didn't stop. And the feelings didn't either. I don't know how many times I orgasmed, how many times I screamed her name. Finally, she crawled up beside me.

"Shhh," she whispered. "Shhh."

I couldn't speak. I couldn't even think. I'd never had an experience like that before. Oh, I'd heard about them but I'd thought they were just someone's fantasy, someone's wishful thinking.

"How did that feel?" I heard her ask.

I shook my head. "Incredible," I gasped softly.

"Want to do it again?"

I took a very deep breath. "I want to do it to you."

I heard her laugh. "Nope. No one does me like that."

"No one?"

"Nope."

"Why?" I couldn't fathom why she wouldn't want something that incredible.

"Because I don't let them."

"Why not?"

She didn't answer but said instead, "I bet you're hungry. I'll get you something. Is there anything in the refrigerator you can't eat?"

"No," I managed to say.

"Don't go anywhere," she said as she got off the bed. I was still tied down. Where would I go?

She made me scrambled eggs and toast and fed them to me while I was still bound to the bed. I was still blindfolded but she was very careful not to spill anything, except . . . I felt food land on my chest but before I could say anything, I felt her suck it into her mouth, ever so slowly.

"Good god," I gasped.

"Like it?" she asked. Her tongue started to lick my body. I'd never had food eaten off me before. It was the most erotic feeling I'd ever felt.

Her lips covered mine. She started all over again. Was I crazy?

I'm not sure how long that lasted.

When I'd relaxed a bit, we started telling each other about our lives. I'm not sure how long we talked or if we even slept but it was midafternoon before we finally got up.

When she untied me and took the blindfold off I asked, "Are you going to visit your sister again any time soon?"

"I have a few three-day weekends coming up, if there's a good reason to be here." She smiled. It was wonderful to see her face. I studied it.

"I can think of a good reason."

"You think?"

I pulled her to me and kissed her. "Reason one: I still haven't had a chance to make love to you."

She laughed lightly, the sweetest laugh I'd ever heard.

"When's your next weekend?" I asked.

"I can be down here in three weeks."

"Then we'll have to make plans. If I put my request in early, I can probably get a day or two off," I told her.

"You mean we could do something besides stay in bed? I may be able to communicate with you more than just waving at the bumps in the ceiling? You want to do something else? You don't want our relationship to be only sexual?" Her face showed wonder.

"That may be the best part." I grinned. "But it's not the only thing."

This time, she pulled me to her and kissed me. And did she kiss me!

I'm surprised I made it to work on time.

That evening I walked into the casino after dropping her off at her sister's. She would be going back to Wichita as soon as she'd showered and spent a little time with her sister. We'd made tentative plans and had exchanged the necessary information; addresses, phone numbers, et cetera. She had said she'd call when she got back home; probably between 3:00 and 3:30 a.m. I said I'd be home by then.

I still couldn't believe everything that had happened, but I was really looking forward to her next visit.

Jane wasted no time in asking how the night had gone. What was I going to tell her? What wouldn't ruin my reputation?

"Did you take her to dinner?" she asked. "Did you go for a drink?"

"Yes, we had something to eat and we talked for a while," I hedged with a shake of my head, "but I got sort of tied up with other things."

FUCK ME LIKE A CANADIAN

Raven Sky

There is a heat to attraction. An energy. You can feel it. It's undeniable. This is the last place I expected to feel it. Not least of all because it's illegal here. Is it punishable by death? I strained to remember my online research predeparture. Morocco. Homosexuality. What did Google have to reveal about that? My mind blanked. Because her hands were on my naked flesh, lathering me in a traditional black olive oil soap. Something in her actions was more than indifferent. Something in her eyes, when they happened to catch mine, was not impersonal.

She put a *kiis* on her hand, a kind of scrubbing glove, and asked me to lie down. I arranged myself on the tile floor, suddenly self-conscious, and she set to work, eradicating days of showerless mountain trekking and sweaty desert camel-riding from my body. It was an odd sensation right on the line between pain and pleasure. I wondered if I should feel embarrassed, but the hammam, the public bath, has no place for modesty. That made me laugh earlier. Seeing Muslim women topless with their hijabs still in place, like modesty had no relation to bare breasts amongst the same sex.

The bath attendant noticed my tattoo, hesitated in her otherwise practiced motions, and asked, "Is this the sign of your people?" I didn't know what to say. The tattoo shows two interlocking women's symbols in rainbow colors, a throwback to my heady first days of coming out. What could I risk here? But she headed me off, lifting a long and silky mane of hair to show her own surprising tattoo gracing the back of her neck. I recognized the symbol. "Berber," she said. "My people." Berbers are the original peoples of Morocco, the first inhabitants who lived here before the Arabs came and colonized. I complimented the design and she smiled. I noticed her eyebrows. Why do women from Muslim cultures often have such perfect fucking eyebrows? Classically arched. Impeccably shaped. 1950s gorgeous. I guess eyes are everything in a culture where hair and bodies are hidden. I tried not to pay attention, to dismiss the obviously electric erotic tension. But this is where it started. This improbable romance between a white tourist and a Berber beauty. Unbelievable.

She complimented my dreads and invited me to a women's party. I knew enough to read between the lines and accepted the invitation with a mix of apprehension and excitement. This was dangerous. And yet I'd never roamed the planet seeking the comfort of the known. The thrill of travel is about stepping outside of everything you know and risking misadventure, and so I went to the party. All women. All gay from what I could glean. A secret underworld of sisters who looked out for one another. I was immediately enthralled.

We fucked for the first time there, Till and I. After a few hours spent drinking wine and singing incomprehensible Berber songs, occasionally dancing with ludicrous abandon, she pulled me into a private room and shut the door meaningfully. The music was turned up outside, and though I spoke another language, I read the signs correctly. She was flushed from dancing, pink-cheeked, eyes afire and I felt suddenly nervous, unsure of what was expected in this new context. But I didn't have to do anything. She was intentional. Stripped for me knowingly, a mocking smile teasing about the corners of her mouth. And I just stood there, mesmerized and slightly drunkenly stupefied, honestly, by the sight of all that undulating tan flesh so enticingly within reach. Her breasts were full and weighty, her stomach achingly round, hips perfect curves. I was overcome. Do I make a move now? I wondered, questioning my role in this foreign interaction, but she left little room for such questions, her fingers working deftly to rid me of my clothing, the last barrier between us.

That night was nothing less than torturous. Till loved every inch of my exterior, caressing, licking, biting, lightly scratching every morsel of my flesh but never entering me. Always careful. I remembered things I'd read in a biography about a Western trekker working his way across the Saharan desert, encountering intimate cultural confusion with Moroccan women along the way, until he learned the unwritten rule that you could play, but you could not penetrate, for that was the prerogative of future husbands. And so he learned to "paint," a not uncommon Middle Eastern form of foreplay, in which a man uses the tip of his penis like a paintbrush to create elaborate patterns upon the beloved's vulva. I remembered this, through clenched jaw and thrusting hips, as Till used the tip of her breast to tantalize me. Her nipples slowly tracing the shape of my lips, spreading wetness into intricate patterns, lulling, maddening, intoxicating, un-fucking-bearable. So close. So fucking enragingly close. I teetered on the precipice of climax until tears sprang to my eyes with the frustration of knowing that it would never happen, not without the hot rush of her fingers inside me. Was it wrong to ask? Was it unthinkable here? Her fingers took over for her ample breast, continuing the maddening artwork, and my whole body trembled on the edge. I couldn't care; I grabbed her by the back of her hair to pull her close and half whispered, half growled, "I want you inside me—please." Her rhythm halted, her face registered surprise, and then a small smile upturned her cheeks and she was inside me. Warmth flooded me, concentrated where she moved within me, and within a few short minutes I was coming loudly as she was laughing and trying to shush me, while the music outside increased rather thoughtfully in volume. That's how we started, Till and I.

What a whirlwind we were. Reckless. Giddy with lust. What she saw in me I was never sure. Was I just a story she would impress the local closet dykes with? A story about her silly fling with a weird-haired foreigner, a white girl she'd managed to seduce? Mind you, was that how I would speak of her, albeit in reverse? Would I similarly reduce this to some tale of an alien dalliance with a mysterious woman from a faraway land? What here was fetishizing the other and what was the pure curiosity of inexplicable, natural attraction? I couldn't say. I just knew that I was enthralled with her and it *was* wrapped up in the differences she embodied.

I'd traveled a lot, hostel hopping from country to country, so I knew the sweet intensity of a vacation romance was partially about its inherently time-limited nature. This could not last and we both knew it. One morning, waking in my impossibly tiny hostel room, she asked me about my plans. I told her I had another week in Morocco and then Essaouira was next on my hope-to-see list. She avoided my eyes, and fiddling with one of my dreads, she mentioned she could take time off from the hammam; that her boss, whose home we had partied at that first night, would understand. She was painfully beautiful in that moment, vulnerable, desirous. I toyed with pushing her boundaries. Watching her face carefully, I teased, "Only if you finally let me fuck you." This had been a struggle from the beginning. Till was generously attentive but always refused to let me return the attention. Many feelings crossed her face in rapid succession but she settled on joy. "Before you leave," she promised and snuggled into me.

And so we said good-bye to bustling Marrakesh, with its scammy snake charmers, transvestite belly dancers, and aggressive street hustlers. We said hello to the seaside, to gulls and open-air cafes and hippie wanderers. We knew our time together was ending, but that just concentrated everything. My second-to-last night, we sat in a seaside bar by the beach and watched boys playing soccer in the sand. We ordered beers. The waiter brought them, but frowned at Till, disapproving. She looked him right in the eye and chugged. I laughed.

"Do you know what my name means?" Till inquired. I shook my head. "It's Tilleli. In Berber that means *freedom*." She laughed. "My mother should have named me more carefully."

I asked about her family but her eyes went hard and she just drank from her beer, so I stared out at the water and wondered about this woman I barely knew. About how in a few days I would be back in Canada where I could be the lesbianest lesbian who every lesbianed and nobody cared, and she'd still be here, hiding, risking her freedom with every encounter. "Do you ever think of leaving?" I asked, after a pause.

"This is my life," she said simply.

I pushed. "Yeah, but you could go somewhere else, somewhere where you could be more free," I insisted. She turned slowly to look at me, the hardness still in her eyes, and said absolutely nothing. She turned back to the water. I'd said something stupid but I didn't know why or what. What did I not understand? I couldn't know.

The last night we fought. There were tears and apologies and I-just-don't-want-you-to-gos. The usual, typical, doomed-romance girl-drama. But it was potent. Emotional tension shifted so easily to sexual tension and she fucked me furiously up against the wall of our little room, fucked me like there was no tomorrow, because there wasn't. Not for us. And when we were done and exhausted, a crumpled sweaty heap on the floor, I saw that she was crying. I never know what to do when women cry. I went to wipe her tears away but she grabbed my hand and held it tightly, looked me in the eyes intently, and said, "I want you to fuck me like a Canadian."

I started to laugh because it was so incongruous, this sudden ludicrous image I had of fucking her up against a snowman. She was wearing only a toque and I was licking maple syrup from her naked, shivering flesh, as a friendly looking moose ambled by. It was stupid and inexplicable and I could see that I was offending her, but I couldn't stop laughing. She threw on clothes and made to leave. I hurried to stop her but she was out the door. I dressed hastily and ran after her. She'd gone to the courtyard. It was after midnight and the air was cool. You could see the night sky just bursting with stars.

I trid to explain. "I'm sorry. I just don't know what you mean by 'like a Canadian.' It confused me and I laughed. I'm sorry."

It was a long-drawn-out affair, but eventually I won her back over and figured out what she meant. She wanted penetration, unusual for non-married women who played here.

"Are you sure?"

"It's not like you'd be the first. Don't be so full of yourself."

Great. Because insults and anger are the way to set the mood. But I knew it was just about me leaving, and so I moved in to make this work.

I grabbed her face in both my hands and forced her to look at me, to stop, to feel the way our breasts were pressed up against one another. I didn't say anything, just waited for her eyes to soften, and when I knew she felt like it, I kissed her. Slow, sweet, holding back, a shy first sort of kiss. I felt her shiver.

We both smiled. I kissed her again, savoring her taste, the warmth of her breath mingling with mine. Her arms were around my waist and my tongue began to dance with hers, so slow, so sweet. I went to lift her shirt. She raised her arms, inviting, and I watched as the fabric rolled across her torso and full breasts, over her head and down to the floor. I brought my mouth close to hers and it opened expectantly, but I didn't kiss her mouth; I touched my lips to her jawline, her neck, her shoulders, her breasts. I lingered there. Cupped the swell of her in my hands and teased her nipples for a time. She shifted her weight and made small noises of pleasure. My hands slipped beneath the waist of her skirt and I pulled it down the length of her legs. In her hasty dressing, there was no time for underthings, and she was magnificently naked.

I looked around for an appropriate space. There was a stray towel by an intricately tiled fountain and I laid it down with extravagant care, smoothing all the corners and acting ridiculously like it was a bed fit for a queen. We both smiled and she approached, knelt on the towel and tried to unbutton me, but I demurred, just as she had done many times before. This was all her. She lay down, her eyes twinkling with a faint hint of daring, her knees up and locked together.

I like to remember her right there. In that moment. In a courtyard in Essaouira. Surrounded by snoring tourists. Just waiting for me to fuck her silly. Looking so utterly tempting in the moonlight. In my memories, I linger here.

In reality, I didn't. I went to town. I'd been waiting so long to touch her that eager would be an understatement. I held her eyes, met their daring, and opened her legs. I feasted on her like a man dying of thirst in the desert feasts at an oasis. I wish I could say I was more suave, more controlled, but I was drunk with delight and abandon. She came before I entered her. So we dallied before take two, losing ourselves in bottomless kisses.

I was deliriously tired. That might have contributed to the random, uninvited images that kept popping into my head as we built up to another go. "Fuck me like a Canadian." It was still funny. This time we were on a frozen pond, hockey players skating all around us, politely averting their eyes as I used my mouth to roll up her rim . . . oh yeah!

That's stupid, stop thinking about that, I told myself. I focused on the task at hand. I had primed her clit sufficiently now, she was slick with desire and now was the time to give her what she wanted. I slipped a finger inside her gingerly. She was tight, but her whole body reacted and I knew it was good. I worked away, patiently, focused, listening intently to her reactions and adjusting my pace and fingers accordingly. Her breath was speeding up, her hips were encouraging a particular rhythm. I kept at it. Now she was peaking, now we were getting there, her hips became more insistent, her sounds more unthinking. But let me tell you, it was a long freaking climb to her summit. My arms began to ache, my fingers to cramp, but I kept on trekking. She was flooding now. I could feel her wetness splashing up my arm, almost to my elbow. I held in there. I kept the beat. I didn't miss a step because I was Canadian goddammit and we were dependable little beavers. The Mountie always got his man. My country was counting on me. She wanted to be fucked like a Canadian, eh? The glory of the maple leaf depended right now on my ability to keep this pumping steady, add just the right twist at just the right moment.

I imagined myself at UN headquarters, Justin Trudeau, with his McDreamy hair and feminist principles, presenting me with a special award for international diplomacy. It came with a life-time supply of Tim-bits and bragging rights as Chief Canuck Pussy Whisperer. k. d. lang would be pissed. *Ha, I out-dyked you,* I gloated inside my head as singing filled the air. Wait, that was real. There was singing. What the fuck?! I looked down at Till and at just that moment her pussy erupted, her muscles clenched and shot out my hand as her body spasmed and her scream joined the singing. I was so confused. Was I that exhausted? My arms felt like floppy spaghetti but was my mind similarly cooked? I fell down beside Till on the sopping-wet towel, shaking all over. That's when I realized it was the call to prayer. The singing. It was the mosque, calling worshippers to the first early morning prayer. So my mind was only half baked. It all made sense.

I love that memory of that ridiculous, gorgeous night, just as I love that sound. And now when I hear it, I think of Till, this beautiful, fierce, brave woman I once had a short time to love. Wherever I am, when I hear the call of the sacred, I think of her.

JANI-LYN'S DRAGON

Nat Burns

September 1970

It didn't matter that she came over unannounced, at odd hours. In fact, I liked it that way. Made it seem more like the illicit, secret rendezvous it was. When I heard the heavy, solid slam of the limo door late that Saturday, I knew it was her and a sense of well-being washed over me. She always affected me that way. I was a Janis-junkie, giving up all hope of any other relationship just for these sporadic, intimate, stolen visits. It was a lonely life. Sometimes I'd see her once in six months, other times three times in one month. I just never knew. Some of it had to do with proximity; if she was playing in a city within one hundred miles she'd point the limo my way. If she was working on either coast, however, I wouldn't see her for a while.

But when she was here . . .

I felt her before I saw her. I stood in the center of my small living room, my breathing shallow. The heat of her presence crept along my back, warming me. Turning my head, I inhaled her unique scent—cigarettes and whisky with an undertone of patchouli. She'd found this lotion once in a little shop outside San Francisco. It was hand-mixed by a woman named Clarence, another of her conquests, I'm sure. She'd been so excited by the new discovery that she'd brought me a whole set of the patchouli toilet water, lotion, and soap. I'd never used them. They were her scent. I did, however, open the bottles often, especially when I was missing her. I'd inhale the fragrance, feeling her all over me. I usually cried.

"Hey, sweetheart," she said from the doorway. "You're gaining some weight finally. You look good!"

I smiled and dropped my eyes, feeling shy. "I always gain a little when the school year begins. All those other teachers bringing in the home-baked goodies to the meetings . . . "

She grinned and placed her woven bag on the hall chair. Then her floppy hat joined the bag, the movement mussing her frizzy auburn hair. I reached into a nearby drawer and fished out a thick, black rubber band from the stack I kept there, just for her.

She took it from me as she moved into the room, her eyes boring into me as if memorizing. I saw the doubt and sadness that was so much a part of her, the familiarity of it soothing me somehow. I think if I'd ever seen true glee in those eyes, I would have known she was an imposter and not my Jani-Lyn.

Our fingers lingered as she took the rubber band from me, then twisted and tucked her hair with big, square hands. I loved those hands and seeing them sent a delicious thrill through my entire body. I well remembered those hands fucking me and moving with tender power across my clit. I almost doubled over from the lurch of sudden desire that filled me.

She knew.

She smiled, her own gaze darkening with wanting me.

After her hair was pulled away from her face and into a reckless ponytail atop her head, I saw my Jani-Lyn. She was no longer the national rock star, hidden behind a cloud of hair, booze, and drugs. She was now, once again, the shy young teen who'd rescued me from the bullying idiots who plagued the halls of Tommy Jeff High School.

Meeting her was a moment I would never forget. I'd been new to the area, my dad transferred by the oil company he worked for. I still hated those unexpected moves, hated having to stand my ground, proving myself at each new school. When Janis stepped in, however, defending me from the band of mischief-seeking rich kids, I found in her a kindred spirit.

The first few weeks after we met were a frenzy of recognition and exploration as we blended into soul mates. We both loved to read and would spend hours discussing the latest bawdy books. We were both redheads, although her hair was much darker, and we both had as many pimples as freckles. We used to laugh, envisioning our white, fish-belly skin as the canvases under dripping brown paintbrushes gone wild. Then we became lovers and found an affinity there, as well.

"And there's my Jani-Lyn," I said aloud.

"Your Jani-Lyn," she agreed, removing her leather jacket and tossing it aside. Underneath it she wore a loose gauzy tunic—stage wear—with the usual long sleeves. She pulled that over her head, revealing a white sleeveless undershirt. This was a privilege, I knew. No one but me saw Janis without her long shirts. Not even her other lovers. Being naked meant being vulnerable, she said. She would fuck them fiercely but always with most of her clothing in place, keeping her power.

I touched her arm, right above the stack of bracelets she wore. I'd given several of them to her over the years. When she shook them onstage, she told me often, it was a special message of love to me. I rotated the arm and gently touched the new track marks amid the scars of the old.

"Jani-Lyn," I scolded, clicking my tongue against my teeth. "I thought you'd let that go, honey. What about Brazil? Getting clean?"

She sighed and pulled me into the arms scarred with her pain. "I did, baby, and it was good. The dragon caught me last week though. I was missing you so much and was stuck out there in Boston. It was hell."

I pulled back and studied her sweet, tired face. She wasn't high tonight. That was good.

I pressed my lips to her neck, inhaling deeply. She always smelled so damned wonderful. Her scent and taste brought far away worlds home to me.

"Ahh," she breathed. "Ahhh, I miss you so much when I'm not here."

Her strong hands moved to my waist and progressed upward until I was caught between her palms. She caressed my ribs and the sides of my breasts, all the while holding me securely. My hands found the belt loops on her low-slung jeans and I tugged them playfully. Her thumbs brushed rhythmically along my breasts, and the heat of her hands consumed my chest.

I found her lips, tasted cigarettes. My tongue felt along the edge of her teeth and frolicked with her tongue. Our bodies pressed closer and her arms moved behind me, each hand caressing my ass. Time passed without our being aware.

"The bedroom," I whispered against her mouth at last.

She kissed me again and then led the way, pulling me along behind. Eagerness made me trip over her and we fell together, luckily onto the mattress. Low lamps provided soft light so I could see her face. I noted that she looked around, making sure her things were still here, always would be here. Her juvenile paintings, and some of the newer psychedelic ones, still papered my walls. Seeing them there always caused her to shake her head in disbelief. I kept the bedroom the way it had always been because I knew it helped us remember.

She slid onto me easily.

Janis knew about kissing, knew that it was the right way to love a woman. Her tongue gently plundered my mouth as her lean body strained against me. I pushed back, wanting so badly to connect. Our clothing melted away in passion's heat, a heat that cocooned us from the world. Soon her thigh was between mine, the rhythmic pressure as she kissed, kissed, kissed me making reality drift farther away on quiet sighs. Her hands found me wet and grasping and she slipped easily inside only to escape and slide against my clit with just the right pressure. I felt the glorious itch grow with her movements until it formed a mushroom cloud of sensation that flared and then dripped billows of whipped cream from toes to head. I fell limp against the pillows, emitting soft moans of pleasure and delighted gratitude.

Her wide, satisfied grin was thoughtful as she studied my face in the dim light.

"I love you, so much," she admitted haltingly.

I pressed my palm to her broad, furrowed forehead, sought her scared eyes with my reassuring gaze. "I know, babe, I know."

She tucked her head and moved lower. Her mouth found me, her tongue strumming the same tune. I held my breath, my fingers holding her shoulders, the tips playing in the hair she'd let grow in her armpits.

Her tongue entered me, stroked me from the inside for a slow-moving century. I felt fingers enter after a millennium and released the held breath. It was too much. When her tongue flicked my clit again, I writhed away, the orgasm so powerful it bordered on pain.

Yet she persisted, and I came once more, screaming and pushing on her shoulders, twisting sideways. I recovered as she breathed heavily between my thighs. I brought her face even with mine. I kissed her hard.

"Let me, Jani-Lyn, let me . . . "

"I told you, baby, I hate that men go there. Sometimes when I'm drunk or high, I don't know . . . stupid."

I reached one hand down and found the softness of her. Her fine hair hugged my hand as I slipped into that hot wetness.

"Oh baby, you are seriously in need," I whispered against her ear.

"Ready, I'm ready," she murmured, those glorious sad eyes closed. I moved lower and pushed in hard and deep, the way she liked it. I watched her face and could see she was into it, she was feeling me. She cleared her throat and one forearm came up to cover her eyes.

"I see you," she said, as if to herself, and I knew she saw the me that turned her on, whatever part of my body or face that did it for her. She never would tell me. Fully focused this way, her body responded to my pushes, meeting each thrust and throbbing inside, tightening against my hand.

"You want it all, baby," I cooed, my voice husky with excitement.

"All," she agreed, nodding.

I loved that I could watch her and she couldn't see my excitement. I could watch the orgasm build in her as I pumped in, pulled out. I slid my hand into a fist. The sudden growth inside sent her gasping so I thumbed her clit with my other hand and repeated the curl. I leaned sideways and latched my mouth on to one of her small, erect breasts, the one with the heart tattoo, and she howled, her body convulsing on my fist. The powerful throbbing of her cunt traveled up my arm.

"Aw, fuck," she whispered some time later. "No one does me like you, baby." She lowered the arm and looked at me, her gaze sated and sleepy.

"I've got mileage," I told her, my voice low and loving. "Lots of miles together with you."

I withdrew my hand gently when the throbbing eased. We snuggled face-to-face, the heated scent of our sex surrounding us, wet warmth gluing our legs together.

"So why didn't you come?" she asked sometime later.

"I did come," I said, half asleep.

"No, today, to the reunion."

I took a deep breath, shifting gears from my sexual high. "I was there. Earlier. Before you came. I almost didn't go at all. I told you, baby. I have nothing in common with those people anymore."

"And I do?" She twisted away to light a cigarette. Fragrant smoke surrounded us.

"No, not necessarily, but you had your own reasons."

"Yeah," she drew on the cigarette, pillowing her head on her forearm. "But maybe not the right ones."

I searched her face, looking for signs of emotional trauma. "What do you mean?"

She stirred restlessly, and I knew she'd be gone soon. "I don't know, man. I don't feel as good as I thought I would."

"Why?" I shifted to see her better.

"They asked all kinds of questions about Mama and all. About growing up here." Her eyes wandered as she sought to escape her feelings.

I frowned. "Not easy stuff, is it?"

"No . . . but Kitty said that Mama told her she was proud of me." Her smile was too hopeful, and it made me sad for her.

"No shit?"

"No shit! Coulda knocked me over with one of my own feathers." She paused. "They still hate me though, all those people in town."

"Don't care about them, Jani-Lyn, care about me, about us."

I sharpened my gaze, making her understand. "What we have is eternal. It's what matters."

She chuckled, amid a cloud of new smoke. "Eternal. I like that."

We cuddled and drifted into sleep. Sometime later I heard her stir. She kissed my cheek while I feigned sleep so there would be no good-byes. But she knew.

I heard the door close, heard her raspy voice rudely waking the limo driver and, no doubt, a few of the neighbors. I smiled and hugged her pillow close.

I never saw her again. The dragon won, carrying her away on powerful wings just a few weeks later.

I think about an afterlife every day. I can only hope there is one and that I will see her there.

RULES

Lea Daley

Pimberly Brauer had prowled through several galleries at the museum seeking a new challenge for her design students before something sparked an idea. An immense, faceted aluminum tapestry by El Anatsui. Its dramatic drapes and folds were composed of tiny, colorful rectangles connected by fine wire. She'd just begun logging notes in her phone when the Associate Dean of Academic Affairs appeared. And there wasn't a colleague at UMKC that Pim liked less. Thea Lincoln was everlastingly oblivious to all social cues. Worse, she was an unrepentant gossip.

Pim stepped closer to the artwork, seeming to study every detail of its superb craftsmanship. Predictably, Thea sidled up anyway. "Hard to believe that's metal, isn't it?"

Outfoxed, Pim turned. "I can barely keep my hands off it."

"Such creativity! People are a never-ending source of amazement—for good *or* ill. Speaking of which, you're well out of that nasty mess with your former girlfriend, aren't you? The latest one, I mean. That preschool program director?"

Plainly Thea was seeking a scoop, but how did she know so

much about Pim's personal life? More importantly, *what* mess? "I don't know what you're talking about."

"That disgusting scandal? Surely you've heard about it. It's been all over the news for the past two days and—"

A scandal? Involving sweet, decent Hayley Walton?

"—now the parents are picketing her school."

Pim longed to flee, but she had to sort out this bullshit. "Why?"

"It seems she abused a student." Thea licked thin lips. "Sexually."

"No way, nohow! You can take that to the bank!"

"Apparently the clients have a different take on young Ms. Walton. They aren't waiting for results from the investigation. They want her gone—yesterday. Check it out, Dr. Brauer." Then, opening a map of the Nelson with a sharp snap, Thea sailed away.

Pim turned back to the shimmering tapestry—a zillion individual elements held in place by the frailest of linkages. Any of which could be severed, perhaps irreparably. Suddenly the thing seemed an analogue of life itself. Sick at heart, Pim walked blindly until she reached an empty gallery. Slumped on a bench there, she let the news sink in: Hayley was in trouble. And she was alone.

Of course, Pim could sidestep whatever madness was afoot simply by maintaining her self-imposed distance. Yet every fond emotion she'd suppressed since dumping Hayley had suddenly come roaring back. All at once, she wanted only to shelter and protect the gorgeous woman that every dyke for miles around must fantasize about. Oh, that slim, athletic body! Oh, those heart-wrenching eyes! Unbidden, a favorite memory surfaced:

Hayley's spread-eagled on Pim's bed. Facedown, honey-colored hair fanned across her shoulders, indigo eyes closed. Pim rubs scented oil over every millimeter of that sleek backside, from the nape of Hayley's long neck to the soles of her shapely feet—and points in between. Stroking. Spreading. Gently probing.

Hayley struggles to turn, cranes to see Pim's face, reaches for a teasing hand. But Pim murmurs, "Not yet. Let it build. Let's make this the best one ever."

Then Hayley's returning the favor. Kneeling, with Pim's legs locked around her neck. Tongue teasing that deep cleft in the dark, dark mass of hair. Promising and withdrawing. Flickering and thrusting. Spinning it out until Pim's begging for release. Hayley can't speak, but her mouth answers. Lips sucking. Teeth nipping. Tongue plunging into the warm, wet, welcoming abyss . . .

A gaggle of rambunctious first graders burst into the gallery. Pim jerked back to reality. She reached reflexively for her phone, but Hayley wouldn't even glance at a text from her, much less answer a call. Pim's only shot at getting through involved cajoling Hayley's thesis advisor, a mutual friend. Thumbing the cell to life, she willed M.J. Gruening to answer.

"Hey," M.J. said—so brusquely that Pim knew she was still pissed. "What's up?"

"I need help contacting Hayley. Please tell her I'm desperate to talk."

"Not happening, Brauer. You had a chance, and you blew it. Don't muddy the waters—especially in the middle of this fucking child abuse investigation. Hayley's already a wreck."

"I can't let her go through that solo, M.J.! I love her! I've been an asshole, but I'm over it. Permanently. She'll take your call. You have to persuade her to see me."

"Ask yourself this: Why in hell would Hayley agree?"

"Because she's cut from finer cloth than I am—and she loves me, too."

A long silence stretched out before M.J. said, "If you hurt that girl again, I'll personally come after you."

"I promise that won't be necessary."

Hayley's cell rang while she was in the preschool's wide-open office, where she was effectively under house arrest, and where every move she made was now viewed with suspicion.

"Hello, M.J.," she said quietly.

"Hi, Hale. You and I should grab lunch soon. Right now, though, I'm calling on Pim's behalf. Please hear me out, okay? Pim wants to get together, but she knew you'd ignore any message she sent."

Willing herself to stay strong, Hayley said, "Thanks but no thanks, M.J. Given current events, I have more than enough madness to manage."

"Which is why Pim's finally able to admit she made a catastrophic mistake. She wants to support you, to be with you."

Hayley fought back tears. "I can't talk about this at work— can't even afford to think about it here. I'll call you tonight."

It was late when Hayley returned that call. After she'd had a tasteless dinner and a long cry. After she'd failed to shake the image of Pim's dancing black eyes, her seductive grin. After her treacherous heart had called up their official introduction . . .

She runs into Pim Brauer, a campus celebrity, at a Friendsgiving potluck hosted by Mary Jo Gruening. Hayley's astonished to learn that Pim already knows her name.

"You're kidding, right?"

"Nope. Of course I know your name. We crossed paths at the university for years."

"Without speaking."

"You were a student then. And much too busy conquering the universe."

"But now?"

"Now you're a graduate, Ms. Walton. So there's no suggestion of impropriety."

"If what?"

"If I take you home for an oral exam."

But they end up at Hayley's place instead. Because it's closer to the preschool, where she'll bike to work after what promises to be a long, exhausting night. Pim explores the public parts of her apartment and Hayley wonders what she thinks of its wicker-and-whitewashed-wood vibe, wonders what will happen when Dr. Brauer spots something familiar in the bedroom—a sensuous lithograph of a nude woman. Which has the professor's own slanting signature in one corner. Of course, Pim doesn't discover that right away. First there's wine. And Adele's smoky voice wafting through warming air. A bit of laughter. And their initial kiss.

Hayley knows Pim has sampled the university's ever-changing smorgasbord of lesbians. Deans. Department chairs. Professors. Visiting professors. Adjunct instructors. Guest lecturers. Coaches—especially coaches. But Pim kisses her with a shy intensity that instantly flares to passion. When Hayley pulls her into the bedroom, the sight of that print, exquisitely framed, almost derails the moment.

"I bought it at the faculty art show last year," Hayley confesses. "I couldn't walk away from it."

"You have excellent taste."

"Yeah," she whispers. "I do."

They're wearing winter clothes: Leather boots with laces a mile long. Thick woolen socks. Jeans. Sweaters. Flannel shirts with tons of buttons. But beneath it all, lacy, lacy lingerie—such a striking contrast to their bulky outer garments. Instead of ripping off everything hastily and diving for the bed, Pim turns each moment into a miniature seduction. Hayley can barely stand now, so Pim's in charge and it seems she's in no hurry tonight. No hurry at all . . .

Hayley shook free of the reverie, furious that she was still so much under Brauer's spell. She fumbled for her phone, punched

M.J.'s number, and said, "I'll meet Pim. Briefly. But somewhere public—a park or cafe, maybe."

"Name it. Pim will be there."

As Hayley approached in Danatella's Ristorante, Pim made the kind of snap assessment every artist relied on. Hayley looked pale, tired, guarded. *And there's a poker face if I ever saw one. A beautiful, beautiful poker face . . .* Pim stood, but had the sense not to reach out.

"Good evening," Hayley said, that formal greeting almost inaudible in the busy restaurant.

She sat, smoothed a napkin over her lap, nodded across the table. "You first."

At the sound of frost in her voice, so many thoughts crowded Pim's brain that she was tongue-tied. *For heaven's sake, you fool, begin with the obvious!*

"Breaking up with you was the dumbest thing I ever did, Hayley. I was a self-centered jerk, and I'm sorrier than I can say. I tried to persuade myself I was protecting you from pain when I was actually fleeing commitment."

"Duh. So what's changed?"

That caustic edge cut deep, told Pim how badly she'd damaged Hayley. She leaned marginally closer. "I got an up-close-and-personal look at life without you . . . and I didn't like it."

"Are you suggesting we pick up where we left off?"

"I'm hoping we can—hoping you'll at least try."

A clueless server materialized, notepad in hand. "Drinks, ladies?"

"Separate checks, please," Hayley said briskly. "I'll have unsweetened iced tea."

"Make that two." *And disappear.*

Ramrod straight on the banquette, Hayley hurled a challenge.

"If you couldn't handle being with me when everything was sunshine and roses, Pim, how will you cope with this shitstorm?"

"Ironically, it's the perfect opportunity to prove how desperately I want a relationship with you."

Pim actually saw it happen—the little crack that opened in Hayley's defenses. "And what would that look like?"

"Whatever you wanted."

Hayley reached for the oversized vinyl folder, opened it, scanned every page as Pim squirmed. "I think I'll have the Caesar salad. And chicken Theresa. And dessert—definitely dessert."

"Dare I hope you're speaking of me?"

"Cool your jets, Dr. Brauer—I haven't decided whether you're even on the menu."

Their server returned, so Pim jabbed randomly at the list of entrees, only wanting him gone. The instant he was out of earshot, she said, "Okay. Since I may not have a chance to talk without an audience, here goes: I love you, Hayley. Truly, madly, deeply, as they say. But I've been trying to bury those feelings."

"Because?"

"Because I was afraid. Mostly of my own weaknesses. I'm used to succeeding at anything I attempt, but I've always ducked one of life's biggest tests—"

"Let me guess: Monogamy. Just one woman in your bed— me—for the rest of your life."

"Until I shoved you away, I didn't think I could handle that. Honestly, Hayley, I meant to be kind. I'd rather die than hurt you."

"And yet you did."

"And yet I did."

"Plus you let me think I'd hurt *you* somehow."

"The thought never crossed my mind, Hale! You were nothing but wonderful, the most wonderful woman I know!" And Pim had known plenty.

Hayley cleared her throat. "Have you been with anyone since you bailed on me?"

"I meant to—that was part of my plan for moving forward."

"And?"

Pim groaned. "I dropped not one, but two, delightful women, quite unceremoniously. Each on our first dates. Because they just weren't you. I think I left skid marks as I bolted from Butches and Babes."

Hayley laughed at the visual, but her smile quickly faded. "And while we were together?"

"Are you asking if I cheated on you? God, no! I never even looked at another woman!"

Hayley leaned forward, well within reach. "Listen up, Pim. I love you, too. Since forever."

Pim gulped tea to keep from kissing those soft, soft lips. "Same here, sweetheart."

"BS, dear doctor." Said with a razor's edge.

Pim found her own hint of metal. "I've loved you since first sighting, Hayley Walton. Come home with me tonight—I need time to talk with you. No messing around, I promise."

"Are you capable of that?"

"On my honor—what little I have. I just want to hold you, to make amends."

"I won't pretend I'm not interested. But I'm in a really ugly jam. Don't sign on unless it's for the long haul. I'm not sure I'd survive losing you a second time."

Pim thrust her chair back, then shot to her feet. "Would Oreos do for dessert? I have a fresh supply. And I want every detail about this absurd abuse charge."

Twenty minutes later, Hayley was curled on Pim's couch, detailing the horror that had suddenly engulfed her life. "It began with a complete nonevent. I took a kid named Felicia Lowry off the playground to remove a splinter from her finger, and never thought about it afterward. But Licia's a whiny, melodramatic kid who doesn't make first aid easy. Apparently someone heard her howling over the security system, heard me talking to her, and called the Abuse Hotline.

"There's no video?"

"Sadly, we weren't in range of a camera—which looks like something I planned, vile creature that I am. The investigator played the audio for me. And though I'm only taking off Licia's mitten, then coaxing her through the extraction, I sound guilty as hell." Tears glittered in Hayley's eyes. "I feel just awful."

"But why? You didn't do anything wrong!"

"You lose confidence pretty fast when even your boss mistrusts you!"

"Did Drew say that?"

"Not exactly. But she wouldn't say she believed me. And she won't allow me near the children."

Pim considered Drew's awkward position. "She's in a tight spot, baby."

"Cold comfort!"

"I'd like to give you some warm comfort—will you let me take you to bed?"

Hayley winced. "I don't think I have the energy tonight."

"I'll just play soft music and massage you till you fall asleep. Things may look brighter in the morning. Because no one could possibly believe you'd harm a child."

"Come check out that picket line. Plenty of people believe it!"

Pim was breaking eggs into a skillet the next morning when she asked what Hayley's lawyer thought about the investigation.

"Lawyer?"

Pim whirled away from the stove. "Tell me you've seen an attorney!"

"Like I could afford that!"

"Well, I can. And I think you need to."

Hayley slipped the spatula from Pim's grasp, flipped an egg. "I like mine over easy, remember?"

Pim snatched the spatula again, waved it fiercely. "I haven't forgotten anything about you, Hayley Walton! Not one damned thing! God knows I tried! I remember the exact shade of your eyes in sunlight, and how they change at dusk. I remember what brand of bike shoes you wear. I remember how your face glows when you hold a baby—and how you hold preschoolers accountable when they act up. I remember the precise angle of your knees when they're wrapped around my neck, remember how your tongue feels on my bare flesh, remember that you go silent just before you come. And I certainly haven't forgotten how you like your bloody breakfast!"

Pim slid eggs from the pan, then jammed a plate into Hayley's hand. "Now stop stonewalling: don't you think you should consult a lawyer?"

Hayley sank onto a chair and stabbed her fork at an egg. "I can survive the first part of the investigation without legal advice. But if the authorities substantiate the accusation, that's a whole new ball game. We'll talk attorneys then. Hopefully it won't come to that." She rose abruptly to scrape her egg and untouched toast into the trash bin. "Sorry. I just can't eat."

"You'll be exonerated," Pim insisted. "Nothing else is possible."

Reentering a relationship with Pim was almost as tough as being dumped by her. Hayley doubted every declaration of affection or commitment. And the first time she tried making love to Pim, Hayley panicked. While smoothing a satin bra strap down Pim's shoulder, she heard her recorded voice saying, "Let me just slip this off so I can take a good look at you."

And when Hayley reached for Pim's breast, that same disembodied voice murmured, "I won't touch you till you're ready." Pushing past the audio flashbacks, past Felicia's phantom wails, she tried to revel in the moment. But as Hayley slid one finger deep inside Pim, she saw that jagged splinter again, remembered asking, "Should I leave it in or take it out?", heard how perverted the question sounded. Then the whole nightmare came crashing down on her, all the humiliation of being suspect, despised, exiled. Hayley flung herself away from Pim. "I can't, sweetheart! I! Just! Can't!"

The second time she tried touching Pim, the same thing happened. And the third.

Now that Pim had reclaimed her ideal woman, she damn well wouldn't let some phony accusation destroy their love life. But Hayley was traumatized, her defenses nearly impregnable. Pim thought about the problem for days before concocting a plan. Maybe it was brilliant. Maybe it was crazy. Just then, though, it was all she had. She reserved a suite for the weekend at an exclusive hotel—an absurdly expensive getaway, since the InterContinental was in walking distance of her condo on the Plaza. But when she drew the drapes that Friday night, there wouldn't be a single reference point for Hayley, nothing familiar. The past would be erased, the future a blank slate. Just the way Pim wanted it.

Hayley agreed to Pim's weekend retreat without asking questions. When they arrived at the hotel, she saw, but didn't register, the magnificent fountain at the entrance. In the lobby, she scarcely glanced at the crystal chandeliers and gleaming marble floors. And she was unmoved by the excellent artwork, the inviting lounge. As the elevator rose, she tried to smile for Pim, who clearly wanted the weekend to be special. But Hayley's attention was fragmented, focused as much on dread as tremulous hope. Pim's plan—whatever it was—might already be doomed.

Upstairs, the accommodations couldn't have been less like the places Hayley spent her ordinary days—the rundown preschool, her own shabby-chic apartment. Everything in the suite was fresh and elegant. Pim had ordered flowers, candles, and a superlative bottle of wine. Halfway through a second glass of merlot, Hayley felt her shoulders relax.

Pim must have noticed. She removed the goblet from Hayley's hand, saying, "In a minute, I'm going to make love to you, baby. But tonight there are rules. *Unbreakable* rules."

Her commanding tone, the suggestive sparkle in her midnight eyes, sent a thrill of anticipation through Hayley. "Rules?"

"Rules. *I* can touch *you*. I can touch *myself*. You can touch yourself—and I might touch you at the same time. But you're not allowed to touch *me*. At all. Anywhere. Do you understand?"

"Yes . . . no!" Even slightly buzzy from that wine, Hayley could have compiled an entire catalogue of emotions: Surprise. Confusion. Curiosity. Excitement. Fear. Even shyness—because Pim had never seen Hayley touch herself. In fact, nobody had seen her touch herself.

Pim cradled Hayley's face between her palms. Kissed her thoroughly. Deflected her questing hands. "Against the *rules*, baby. Sit there. Watch me."

Hayley fell onto the love seat, heart racing.

Pim began to speak, her voice conversational. "I started masturbating when I was ten. I didn't have a clue what I was doing." One hand was circling the silk shirt over a breast, the other caressing the fabric between her legs. "I liked feeling myself through my clothes, but soon that wasn't enough."

Pim stepped out of her slacks, unbuttoned that shirt. Then both palms were moving beneath her bra and she was moaning a little.

She slipped one hand inside her thong, but only for a second. When she withdrew it, her fingers glistened. "Before long, I learned how to make use of this," she said, tracing a slippery thumb across Hayley's lips, sliding it into her mouth. "You can touch yourself, darling. As if you were alone . . . "

Then Pim tossed her thong to the floor and lifted one foot to the desk chair. Hayley could see a dense wedge of ebony hair bisected by pink, pink folds. The pathway into Pim. Who was spreading herself wide.

Warmed by more than merlot, Hayley shrugged off her shirt and pants, then collapsed on the love seat again. Where she shoved her bikinis down and pushed her bra up until her breasts jutted outward. Toying with her nipples, she watched Pim. Watched Pim watch *her*. Watched Pim match movement for movement. Groaning, Hayley parted her own flesh, begged to be touched.

"No—I want to watch you. Want to feel myself, as if I were feeling you. Want to see what you look like when you make yourself come."

Soon Hayley's fingers were almost a blur, and Pim was crying, "Do it, darling, do it for yourself. Show me what feels good, what feels best." And all the while, she was flicking her own nipples with her nails, stroking her clit till her knees gave out, then clinging to the back of that chair as she came and came and came.

Then Pim was crawling across the carpet, eyes on Hayley, pulling those bikinis all the way off. Blowing gently on every sensitive part. Lapping relentlessly. And when at last Hayley was done, Pim told her she wasn't. "Because I *know* you. Because I've seen what you're capable of. Because I know how much you love this."

She drew Hayley to the floor and rolled her facedown. Unhooked her bra. Tucked Hayley's hand into that deep, wet rift. Lay atop her. Reached beneath to find those urgent nipples. "This time do it harder," Pim demanded. "I want to feel you come under me. Want you to rock my world while I play with your tits, while I come against your thigh."

Soon Hayley was bucking under Pim, crying, *"Fuck me! Please fuck me!"*

But Pim said, "You do it, baby. Show me how it's done, make me come, make me come now!" So Hayley fingered her clit as she lifted her ass again and again, thudding against the carpet. When she screamed in release, Pim let her rest awhile. Just a little while.

Until she turned Hayley on her back. Tucked one pillow gently under her head and two beneath her rear. "The first time I masturbated with another girl, we did it this way. She was propped on pillows, like you are, and I said, 'Open yourself for me.' And she did. But slowly. In stages. First she licked her fingers till they were dripping, then she frosted herself with that moisture. Yes, Hayley, exactly—that's right! Next she told me to stroke my breasts while she showed me her clit. 'Touch that,' she told me. 'Now find yours and work it between your fingers.' Then she said, 'Sometimes I put something inside myself, but I only want you to use your hand. One hand, while the other plays with your nipples.' I did all that— just the way *you* are now, but finally I had to fall on her, my lips on her lower ones, like this."

Maddened, Hayley writhed and arched, but Pim drew back, spoke softly. "She held my face hard to her there, till she had no choice but to come. When *I* came seconds after, my own fingers were so far inside me I thought I'd found the gates of paradise. Yes! Exactly the way you're doing, *just* like that! Don't stop, love—you're almost there! But no, don't touch me. It's not allowed tonight.

"Watch, I'll do it myself, Hayley. For you. Everything you've wondered about, everything you'd like to know, all the questions answered because I'm showing you exactly what I like, exactly what works, just how I fuck myself when no one's watching,

when there's no hurry, when no one else matters. And sometimes I like to take it slow, just barely touch my nipples, but, no,
darling—put your hand down—the *rules*. Better yet, put it on
you, light as a shadow, light as my breath, breath you can barely
feel, but cooling, so you have chills now and your nipples are
so hard. They could only be harder if I pinch them like this. But
biting's better, Hayley, sharper, you feel it straight in your crotch,
don't you, and I'm going to put my mouth there, right where
you're throbbing . . .

"But you can't touch me, which is too bad, because I'm throbbing too, and I'm going to have to touch myself for a few minutes.
You can watch, but here's your hand on you again, and we can do
it together. And when I come, you'll say I'm beautiful, and I'll say
you are, too, because I see you're coming now, a tsunami racing up
your thighs and slamming into your clit, over and over. And you're
the most beautiful thing I've ever *seen*, Hayley Walton!

"And, yes, I want your mouth on me, your tongue inside and
everywhere. Want you to slip a finger into my ass, but you can't do
that tonight, because tonight there are rules. And rules are rules.
But I can come just looking at *you* coming, sweetheart, so that's
all right. And we're both so tired, but we feel so good, don't we,
just pulsing with the thrill of it all? And sometime maybe the rules
will change, but not tonight, so you'll just have to be satisfied with
your own hands right now, just have to get off on the sight of my
wet, wet fingers pumping in and out of me, and circling my clit.
And maybe tomorrow the rules will be different, but right now,
I want you to pinch your nipples hard, harder, *yes*, because I see
how much that excites you.

"And when you've made yourself so hungry for my touch that
you think you'll go mad without it, then I'm going to take over,
and my mouth will be a soft comfort on your aching breasts and
you'll rock against me, but I can't let you touch me, because you

have to follow the rules. Oh, *yes!* That's it, that's it, come just like that, just like that, yes! Until the rules change—"

"*Pim!*"

"Baby?"

"It's after midnight."

"Tomorrow already?"

"Tomorrow, Pim! Another day. There are new rules now! And those rules say I can touch you, but you can't touch me."

"I'll die if I can't touch you, Hayley!"

"You won't, because I won't let you. Because I'm not through with you yet. I'm She-Who-Must-Be-Obeyed and I'm only getting started!"

Much later, when Hayley had finally recovered, she reached again for Pim. Touched her without rules. Without restraints. With only deep longing. And found that all her phobias had fled. Nestling into the woman she loved, Hayley whispered, "I think I'm beginning to understand why they call you 'doctor.'"

PERFUME

R. D. Miller

It's our fifth anniversary. Five years I've been with this woman; she's beautiful, kind, and intelligent. There are plenty of days when I wonder how she ended up with a dumb butch like me, but when she looks at me she smiles like I'm an unexpected rainbow in the sky. Before her I was lucky if my relationships lasted six months, so it's hard for me to believe that she's still by my side; even harder to believe that I'm still by hers. I was mostly the fuck and run type; maybe I'd make a lady breakfast in the morning, but that was usually as far as it went. This year I wanted to show her what a fucking miracle she is, so I planned a trip to the South of France. My friends told me I was a fool not to take her to Paris. I shrugged and said, "I got this."

See, I know her; I have studied and learned her in ways it had never even occurred to me to be curious about before. She has this thing about perfume. She says she got it from her mother who taught her how to apply it, *just so,* in all the right places to attract men. She dabs it into her belly button to diffuse it with her body heat. She adorns the back of her hands so when she gestures it leaves a trail of scent in the air, drawing people in. The first time she told me that story she giggled like a maniac at the irony of her mom insisting perfume would land her a good man. I fell in love then and there. Who knows, perhaps it had something to do with the perfume that wafted off her skin; hints of jasmine over a sandalwood base. It drew me in, made me want to be closer, made me want to touch her.

On our one-year anniversary she confessed she thought that me falling for her had everything to do with her perfume. I insisted that perfume had nothing to do with it, that I had fallen for her smile, her laugh, her lips that I couldn't stop staring at, couldn't stop wanting to kiss. Those lips that I *still* can't stop wanting to kiss. She arched her eyebrow and told me she believed her mother's words; her scent had captured me, and she intended to keep me. Then she kissed me, and all I could think was how happy I was to be kept.

So I brought her here to Grasse, France, the perfume capital of the world. Where seventeenth-century stone buildings rise up on the hills and narrow cobblestone alleys hold delightful crêperies, colorful cafes, and tiny perfume shops. There are countless fields of jasmine and May rose surrounding the town and the intoxicating smell of flowers permeates the fresh mountain air. From the square in the old town center you can see the ocean; it's only fifteen kilometers to Cannes and the Côte d'Azur. She was so excited when we arrived. She delighted in exploring, her eyes shone as she took in every vista, every alley, every charming little shop. She smiled at me like I was a field of lavender in full bloom.

It's late June, solstice is upon us, and in France that means it's time for Fête de la Musique. It's a night filled with live music everywhere; every street corner, every square, every balcony fills with the sounds of music, dancing, and laughter. Before we left home, we had decided that we would be open to adventure, to exploring and being in the moment, with Fête de la Musique and perfume our only itinerary.

As part of our vacation, I arranged for us to tour all three of the largest perfumeries in Grasse, and today was the first. It was a fairly quiet day in this ancient village; most of the tourists had already left in anticipation of the nighttime festivities in nearby Nice, Antibes, and Cannes. We pulled our rental into the nearly empty parking lot and she was bouncing in her seat. I'd never seen anyone so excited about perfume.

We went in and met our tour guide, a tall brunette with big brown eyes, and curves that made the highway to Monaco look like a straight shot through the desert. We were the only two visitors scheduled for her English language morning tour, she explained as she stepped between us. She boldly linked her arms through ours and ushered us into the museum to start the tour. She led us through leisurely, teaching us about the history of perfume, the company, and the building. She told us about the art form of creating scent and the science of making it stay. My girlfriend was mesmerized by the whole process. She marveled over the large stainless steel vats, read every explanation on every exhibit, gasped in surprise when she heard that it takes three tons of flowers to get just one liter of essential oil. She hung on every word the guide said.

I admit I may have missed a sentence or two, distracted by the tactile nature of our very friendly guide. As the tour continued, her smile became more flirtatious and her touch more frequent. She particularly liked to touch and squeeze my forearms when she was making a point; she must know what that does to a butch. I laughed it off, and I thought my girlfriend did too. I chatted amicably with her as the tour continued and easily developed a friendly rapport.

Halfway through the tour, our guide suddenly pulled a pen out of her pocket and wrote her number on a scent-soaked fragrance strip. She had just used it to demonstrate a musk that she swore was an aphrodisiac; she claimed that it could win over even the most stubborn of hearts. As she scribbled down her number she told us excitedly about a medieval village not far from Grasse. Tonight, for Fête de la Musique, there would be an all-female punk band playing in the courtyard of a small castle. She told us about a charming inn nearby where we could sleep, and that she would be there with her friends; she hoped we'd join them. She held eye contact with me as she pressed the musk-scented strip of paper into my hand and her touch lingered as she moved forward to continue the tour. I was certain her body brushing against mine as she moved past was purposeful. I thought it was funny. I guess I think it's obvious to everyone that I'm so *very* unavailable; perhaps not.

As the guide moved on ahead I turned to my girlfriend and excitedly began talking about the punk band. Watching an all-female band playing at a medieval castle was pretty high on my list of best fucking things to do on a vacation, ever! She didn't reply as I kept rambling on about the castle, just turned and followed our guide as we were led farther into the perfumery.

We're in the gift shop now and I have finally figured out that my girlfriend is feeling jealous. I can tell she's mad by how straight her spine is, her severe glances, and the sharply polite responses she gives as we explore the shop. I reach for her, to rest my hand casually on her hip, to let her know I'm not swayed by the number in my pocket, or the sexy French accent. She moves away too quickly, and it's obvious that she doesn't want my touch right now. Jealousy, possessiveness, totally not her thing; but for some reason this curvy brunette tour guide has her on edge. I know she's trying to find something nice for her mother; that was one of the reasons she wanted to come here. I decide that in this mood she'll browse better if I'm out of her way, so I excuse myself and go to the washroom.

I enter the women's restroom and stop to look in the mirror for a minute. I laugh to myself at my girlfriend's jealousy. I tousle my short hair a bit in a halfhearted attempt to tame it before giving up; it's pretty unruly anyway. I splash some water on my face and wonder how long I should stay in here. As I contemplate, the door behind me opens rather suddenly and she sweeps in, all fire and edge. Her voice is low, a growling, demanding tone that makes my stomach drop. "Stall! Now!"

I'm not sure what's happening, but my god she's beautiful. Her face is flushed, her eyes flashing dangerously, teeth bared when I hesitate to obey. "Now!" That one word is spoken with such authority that I don't think, I obey immediately and walk into the far stall. She's right behind me, stalking her prey.

As soon as we're inside she quickly shuts the door and locks it. I turn toward her and before I can speak, question, or smile, she's on me. She pushes me up against the bathroom wall, her eyes pools of black, pupils blown wide. My mouth goes dry. It seems all the moisture is needed elsewhere. Her hands are on my hips immediately, and her perfect lips are at my ear. Her warm breath sends a shiver down my spine. "You like the sexy French girl, do you? You want to fuck her? Hear her pretty little mouth call your name?"

I'm caught off guard by the vulgarity. Not that I mind, but it's so unlike her. I open my mouth to tell her no, I don't want to fuck the sexy French girl, I only want to fuck her. But before I can say a word, my mouth is full of her tongue. She kisses me; it's rough, deep, full of fire. She pulls back, leaving me breathless. Her hands move to my waist, urgently tugging the end of my belt free from the keeper, unfastening it.

"It looks like you need to be reminded whose girl you are," she growls in my ear. "Who you belong to." She isn't normally jealous, and she hates when women are treated like possessions. I know I shouldn't find this hot, but my god she's sexy like this—commanding, dominant.

My pants are unfastened now and she roughly shoves her hand down them. She pauses, just long enough for her eyes to lock with mine and check for consent. I'm nodding like a madwoman, praying she doesn't stop.

She must be satisfied with that because her hand is suddenly inside of my underwear, and I am dripping for her. She gasps. She bites my earlobe, says, "You are so wet! My butch likes being shoved against the bathroom stall and fucked, does she?" She slides two of her long, talented fingers deep inside me. I try to stay quiet but I hear a keening moan and realize it's coming from me. She slides her fingers in and out, brushing over my G-spot every time. She knows every centimeter of my body by now; she knows how to play me. She knows I'm practically gone, she knows; and so she stops, withdraws. Suddenly I feel so empty, so wretchedly forlorn at the loss of her fingers. I whimper.

"Are you wet for me? Or is this for the fucking tour guide? Answer me!" Her breath is hot in my ear.

"You! Always you," I manage to choke out, desperate for her to continue.

"I'm not convinced," she replies. "You thought she was hot. You flirted, you took her number."

"I . . . the concert, I . . . castle, I . . . please, baby." My frustration is growing. I can feel her fingers toying with me, circling the opening of my vagina, tormenting me with pressure too light to be friction. Her breasts are pressed tightly against my chest, her breath teasing my ear.

"Please what?" She dips her fingers inside, barely, just enough to make me whine again.

"Please . . . please fuck me . . . " I'm beyond caring, I'll beg, I'll do whatever she asks if she'll just keep fucking me in this bathroom stall, in the gift shop of this perfume factory, in this lovely fucking provincial town that always smells of flowers. I'm sure I'll laugh at the imagery later, but for now I can't think about anything but her fingers.

She sinks in farther, to her knuckles. I breathe out, unsteady, shaken, needy. She smirks. "You want the French girl?"

"No! Fuck! You know I only want you!" My hips have grown a mind of their own; I'm humping at her fingers, desperately searching for more friction.

"Whose girl are you?" she demands as she thrusts all the way in, drawing a yelp of both surprise and delight from my lips.

"Yours." I moan. She thrusts again. "Yours." She twirls her wrist and moves her dexterous fingers, pressing them up into my slick walls. "Fuck! I'm yours." She picks up her pace, and presses the heel of her hand into my clit. "I'm yours! Only yours."

I hear the bathroom door open, the click of heels on the tile floor. I know she hears it too, but she doesn't stop; she wants them all to know whose girl I am. She wants them to know she's fucking *her* fine butch in their bathroom. I'd likely be embarrassed if I could form coherent thoughts, but all I can see, smell, feel is her; her fire, her passion, her.

A tap turns on, the water runs; she bites down on my earlobe and swirls her fingers just so, just the way I like. I bite my lip to hold back a moan but it still escapes. It energizes her and she adds a third finger. I suck my breath in and gasp in pleasure. The tap turns off, I hear a soft giggle and the sound of heels retreating. The door opens and closes again.

"Fuck, baby, she heard us!" I'm half expecting a security guard to run in and arrest us or something.

"Good." Her voice is rough, low, dangerous. I feel myself get even wetter, impossibly wet. "Mmmm, you like me fucking you like this, don't you?" I tilt my head back, concentrate on her fingers. "Answer me!" She bites me again, and another moan escapes.

"Yes! Fuck, yes!" My answer rushes out and curls around her ears. She grins, a wolfish, carnivorous grin that I don't see often. She's usually soft, lovely, beautiful. Our sex life is very mutual, except when we get rough. When we fuck, I fuck her. When we play, she submits to me. But sometimes . . . sometimes, fuck, sometimes . . .

She sets to work, skillful fingers playing me like an instrument. With just a few more pumps, a few more swirls of her wrist, she has me teetering on the edge. My body is tight and rigid, my throat exposed as I tilt my head back.

She licks my neck where the skin is taut against the rushing blood. She can taste my pulse. She burrows down, finds the edge of my collarbone and bites down. As she bites she presses her hand hard into my clit and pushes her fingers up against my G-spot. I come. I fucking explode! I'm loud but brief as I cling to her, my short, neatly clipped nails digging into her skin.

I'm panting for breath and she's smiling, smiling like this is the best ride at the amusement park, smiling like I'm the fucking sun. "Whose girl are you?" she whispers, softly.

"Yours. Holy fuck, I'm yours." I'm panting, leaning against the wall because I think my knees might buckle if I move. She slowly removes her hand, brings it to her mouth, and licks me from her fingers. I tremble with desire as I watch her and my voice squeaks as I try to speak: "Always yours."

She looks smug as I struggle to compose myself. "That's right, baby girl. You're mine." She leans in and kisses me; it's soft, gentle, full of love.

When she steps away I miss her immediately, but she smiles brightly. "We'd better get out of here before they send security in after us, no? I have to find something for Mom, and the candles here just smell so lovely! We should get a few. Plus, we have to find that little inn Gabrielle told us about near the concert tonight; you know we'll both have some drinks, so we'll have to stay over."

I'm at a loss; the transformation is so sudden. Her edges are soft again, the searing heat is back to a radiating warmth. I blink stupidly as she leans in and kisses me softly on the lips. She smiles, and even blushes as she glances down at the disheveled mess her butch girl-friend is in, standing against the wall in this bathroom stall.

"Besides, it looks like you're going to need some cleanup time before dinner." She winks mischievously at me. I sputter an attempt at answering as she turns and struts out of the stall. She doesn't stop to wash me off of her fingers and before she exits she throws a pointed look back over her shoulder, instructing me to hurry.

A few minutes later I come out of the bathroom and see her paying for a pile of candles and a nice bottle of perfume for her mom. She's smiling and laughing with Gabrielle, the tour guide. I approach and get a once-over from both of them, and Gabrielle laughs and blushes knowingly. I sputter yet again, wondering where my butch cool went as I try to make an excuse for taking so long in the bathroom.

She laughs at me, smirking as she offers a friendly handshake to Gabrielle, the hand she just fucked me with; one last display of dominance. Then she slips her arm around my waist and steers me toward the door, telling Gabrielle we'll see her later as she whisks me out of the perfumery.

TRYING SUBMISSION

Xan West

From *Shocking Violet*

Liliana was glad she got to the restaurant first. She picked out a table near the bathroom where she could have her back against the wall and watch for Roz to arrive. She'd spent all afternoon figuring out what to wear, before settling on her denim mini, music note leggings, Ursula T-shirt with the neck cut out, leather jacket, and Docs. She'd agonized over how to wear her hair (two braids so she could wear a hat and scarf and wouldn't fuck it up), and how to do her makeup (cat-eye with purple lipstick so dark it was almost black). She'd already made this date into a huge deal in her head and Roz hadn't even arrived. Liliana grabbed her cane in both hands and pressed it into the floor, trying to settle. She closed her eyes, taking a slow breath. When she opened them, Roz was there, smiling down at her.

Her smile was spectacular; it made her eyes go all crinkly at the edges. Her hair was short and natural, her eyes accented with royal blue, her lips a deep, dark red. Roz wore jeans that seemed painted on, with this floaty teal blouse that bared her gorgeous shoulders, and draped to perfection. Silver hoops dangled from her ears. Liliana couldn't help the smile that cracked her usually stoic face. She wasn't even sure she wanted to. Roz was utterly magnificent, and her presence just wrapped Liliana up, made her feel both fluttery and certain.

Roz asked if a hug was okay, and Liliana nodded, putting her cane aside. Liliana rarely felt small, she was too tall and fat for that to happen much. Roz wasn't actually bigger or fatter than her, but somehow, with Roz's solid arms holding her, dammit she felt *vulnerable*. The hug was exactly what she needed, probably too much of it, because her eyes began to sting and her heart started racing. Then it was over, and Liliana picked up the menu, trying to get her heart to slow down, to get herself under control. When it was time to order, she barely got the words out. Her damn heart wouldn't slow down, either. She excused herself and made her way to the bathroom.

Liliana's shields must be leaking. That had to be it. And that needed to be tended to right away. She could do this. It was no big deal. She had time. Roz would wait. This was a single stall bathroom, so no one would fuck with her. That was why she'd suggested this restaurant, which was close to empty, even on a Saturday night. Well, that, and the armless sturdy chairs. No sense taking another fat woman to a place where neither of them could sit comfortably.

Liliana turned on the faucet, let the water flow. Ran it over her hands, drawing from it to strengthen her shields. She grasped for the vision in her mind, herself as an octopus, all purple-black tentacles and massive strength, checked each arm mentally, running water over every inch. Supple, fast, strong, that was what she needed to be. She breathed in, holding that intention.

No leaks allowed. She might feel all quivery and tender underneath, but she wasn't going to damn well show that to anybody.

Liliana repaired her face slowly, deliberately. Applied her inky purple lipstick exactly right, like the color was helping to sink octopus strength into her. Took her time because she was in charge of herself, dammit.

Then she grabbed her cane and slowly strolled back to the table, shields in place, ready to ask for what she wanted like it was no big deal. Acting casual about things she needed too much was her specialty.

She could feel Roz's eyes on her. Roz seemed to be watching all the time, tracking everything. Liliana did that too, but this felt different. Roz's eyes on her, there was a weight to them. The weight was comforting, like her blanket at home. It was also . . . yeah, *juicy* was the best word.

She could feel herself sitting up straighter, because she was under Roz's gaze. She was more aware of her skin, of how close Roz's boots were, under the table. Aware that if she moved her foot just so, they'd be touching. She didn't move her foot. She just became extremely aware that she could, aware that Roz was just a few tiny inches away.

"Hey there, darlin'. You gonna talk to me, hmm?" Roz's voice was husky and teasing. Like she knew what Liliana was going to ask.

Liliana raised her eyes to meet Roz's for a second, and whoa. If her eyes felt powerful on Liliana's skin, they were on a whole other level this way. Not just because Liliana rarely made eye contact with anyone. They jolted right through her, and held her in place, breathless and spinning. She was dizzy from just that momentary glance up.

"Yes. I'll talk to you," she got out.

"Mmm. Good. Tell me what you have in mind, then. Your latest text implied you wanted to ask me something."

Liliana gulped. She just got right to the fucking point, didn't she? And only after she got Liliana to promise to talk about it. How the fuck did she get backed into a wall already?

"Umm. Okay. I. I would like to do a scene, if you were into that."

"And what kind of scene were you wanting, hmm?"

Okay. Best if she said it fast. She took a drink of water, first. The water was cold in her hands, and that was good.

"I want to try submission," she said, as fast as she could get it out.

"Submission." Roz seemed to taste the word, roll it around her tongue. "You want to try submission. Have you tried submission before?"

"No, I haven't," she said softly. "I've just thought about it."

"Mmm-hmm. How long have you been thinking about it?"

Liliana sighed. "A very long time." She wanted to say ma'am at the end of that sentence, but wasn't sure if that was right. And would that be confusing? Violet was Ma'am, but the ma'am she wanted to say was different, would be different. Maybe it wasn't even the right word. Maybe she didn't have the right to say it. Maybe she had to earn that.

It was better to be careful, she decided. She'd heard tops complain at Femme Brunch, about the ways that bottoms took liberties, just decided they could use words like that. She didn't want to take liberties. Roz hadn't even said she was interested. She hadn't said no, so maybe that meant she was. But Liliana didn't want to assume.

"What made you choose me?"

Liliana's heart started racing again. She pulled the fidget out of the pocket of her leather jacket. Yes, this helped. The coolness of the metal, the smoothness, the way it moved all even.

"I trust you. Violet trusts you. When you hug me, I feel . . . held. Like it's okay for me to take down my guard. When I look at you, I feel awed. Breathless," she said hoarsely. Then she drank some water before continuing to list her reasons. "I don't need to explain stimming or going nonverbal or any of my autistic stuff, you already know. You're in our leather family, and that feels right, to try this with family first. It feels . . . less fraught to try this with another woman of color. I know you wouldn't go easy on me. I want to really try this." She swallowed, looked up to meet Roz's gaze again. "And I feel it, already. The possibility of D/s, between us," she said.

"Yes," Roz said simply. "I feel it too. And I get it, about wanting someone you know and are already connected to, where there's more trust, and safety. About wanting to try it with another woman of color. Though I generally call myself Black."

Liliana nodded, then looked down again. Roz's gaze was so much. She couldn't hold it anymore.

"I use Latina, most of the time. In some situations I call myself a trans woman of color," she offered.

"I'm honored that you trust me, Liliana. I will admit, I *have* wondered what you might be like, if you submitted. When I got your text, I hoped you might ask to play. Talked it over with my girl this afternoon. She thought we might suit, and I gotta say, I agree. The chemistry is there."

Liliana nodded, then put the fidget down to drink some water.

"So, let's talk about what this could look like," Roz said. "A scene, you said. Perhaps at Lilith's, where I'm staying? On Saturday. Nobody will be there. Lilith is out of town. My girl is staying with her momma that night."

"That sounds good."

"When you've thought about it . . . what are the things that you think about? What does it look like?"

Liliana felt frozen. Couldn't get her mouth to open. Her hands started fluttering.

"Okay. That's a hard question. That's just fine. How about this? I'm going to ask you some things and you nod if it's yes and shake your head if it's no."

Liliana nodded. She could do that.

"Being at my feet."

Yes.

"Bondage."

No.

"My hand on the back of your neck."

Yes, please.

"Being used."

No.

"Being treasured."

Oh yes.

"Being punished."

Nope nope nope.

"Being useful."

Yes yes yes yes yes.

"Calling me Ma'am."

Yes. Most definitely yes.

"Sexual service."

No. Just, no. Not for a one-night scene.

"Sex."

No. Not tonight.

"Taking pain because I need to give it to you."

YES.

"Taking your shirt off."

Yes.

"Being naked."

NO.

"Letting go of control, and letting me make the decisions during the scene."

Yes. It scared the shit out of her but ohhh yes.

"Being called girl."

Yes.

"Okay, girl. That should be just fine," Roz said softly. "I'm looking forward to this."

Liliana smiled. Her hands were slowing down. It felt good to be called girl. She drank some more water.

"Me too, Ma'am," she said, her voice barely audible, the word Ma'am sweet on her lips, exactly as she'd hoped it would be.

"Okay then. Next Saturday good for you?"

Liliana nodded.

"Let's get out of here," Roz said briskly. "How about you tell them to wrap the rest of this up, while I use the restroom."

Liliana nodded, sat up a little straighter. She had them bring the containers to her, so she could box things up herself. She wanted to make sure it was done right. It felt good to have something concrete to do. She could feel herself getting calmer, and more focused.

She texted Violet: *Leaving the restaurant now. Roz agreed to play, we have a date next week. Will be home soon.* Violet responded. *Okay, girl. Enjoy! I'm at Pam's tonight. See you in the morning.*

This was a good plan. She was ready. Well, as ready as she was going to be to try something she'd been fantasizing about forever.

Liliana's heart was pounding in her throat. She was actually going to do this. Once her coat was off she just stood there. She didn't know what to do with her hands. One was holding her cane but the other one was fluttering and that was probably okay. It had been okay at the restaurant so she knew it was okay and she just needed to fucking chill but she couldn't. So she just stood there and waited. Hoping Roz liked the fat pride T-shirt, denim vest, pink tulle skirt, and black leggings she'd decided to wear tonight. Hoping that Roz would tell her what to do. Hoping she'd get to sit soon, her knee was not happy right now. Was the scene starting, had it already started?

"How about you sit down on the couch, girl. We've got a few other things to see to before we get started."

Liliana nodded. She could do that. The couch was kind of fancy. Actually the whole place was real fancy. This Lilith person had to be fucking wealthy. So much space, and in Manhattan too? There was this huge skylight, and was that a loft bed? Huh. Roz looked completely at home, here, her boots up on the coffee table, her arm slung over the back of the couch. But had she ever seen Roz when she didn't seem like she owned the entire room? Liliana was nervous at how fancy everything was. What was she doing here? She'd probably knock over something priceless and it would shatter.

"Girl, you look like a cat whose fur was rubbed the wrong way. What's up?"

"I've never been in a place like this."

"Ah. Yes, it *is* something. Took me a while to actually feel comfortable. Yeah, white people like Lilith, who come from old money, are at this whole other level, girl. I get it. It's hard to figure out how to be here."

Liliana nodded. She felt like she needed to be really still and not touch anything.

"If it helps, Lilith really does want me to make myself at home. She'd be happy to know I brought a girl home with me who wanted to try submission for the first time. She would want you to feel like her home was a safe space to try that."

It was a surreal space to even imagine being unguarded in. But maybe that might work. Like this was an alternate universe or something. Because she couldn't ever imagine living in this place, or even visiting frequently. Maybe it would make her more brave?

She wanted this with Roz, but it was separate from her life in a lot of ways. That's what made it safe enough to ask for. Roz lived in Toronto, and while she visited a few times a year, this couldn't be something serious. The scene happening in a place like this was just another way that was true. Alternate Universe Liliana could go for it because this was taking place in a separate sphere.

She smiled at Roz, nodded. Waited to see what came next.

"I've got something for you to look at, before we start."

Liliana nodded and began reading. Oh this was good. This made it easier. She read the list of Roz's limits three times, repeating them in her head so they would stick. She looked at the nonverbal safeword for a long time. Then she decided to ask. She got Roz's attention, and pointed to it, held her hand out over the couch between them, and tapped three times.

"Yes, that's right," Roz said. "You can also do that on my body. Try it on my thigh, right here."

Liliana gulped. She was going to touch her. Okay. She tried it. Roz was warm, she could feel it through the smooth cool fabric of her dress. And solid. She felt so solid.

"Yes, that's good. Better to have a nonverbal one from the start, I think. Though if you can access words, I'll check in if you say stop, or red. But this way you don't need to try to push through for words."

Liliana smiled at her. She suddenly felt all full of gladness. It was a brilliant shining thing to know that she could try this and it would really be okay to go nonverbal. As long as she could tap out, she was okay being where she actually was at. She could do this, could tap out before she lost all communication. She trusted herself with that. It would be good to be Alternate Universe Liliana for the night.

"So I know you have fibro, and use a cane to get around. Can you tell about the kinds of things you can or can't do, physically?"

She could push through for words with this. She breathed, thought about it.

"I can stand for a few minutes without the cane, but not long. I can sit and lie down no problem."

"How are your hands? Can you do things with your hands? Massage, ironing, anything like that?"

"Yes, Ma'am. My hands aren't hurting tonight."

"All right. You said you wanted to be at my feet. Are you able to sit on the floor?"

"No, Ma'am."

"Okay. What would give you the feeling of being at my feet? If I'm standing behind you while you are sitting? If you are lying at my feet while I sit on the couch? I don't think the loft bed is accessible."

Liliana nodded. She agreed, it didn't look like it with that ladder. "The couch, maybe."

"Okay we'll try it and see. In fact, let's start with that, girl."

"Yes, Ma'am."

Roz moved to the end of the couch. She took her beautiful boots off, sighed, then took her socks off too. Her toenails were teal and royal blue. Peacock colors, like she was wearing on her eyes, like the royal-blue dress hugging her curves, like the necklace that was drawing attention just so to her cleavage in that plunging neckline. Liliana loved femmes so much, loved picking out the details that showed the incredible care Roz took to show off her plumage. She had worn her fine feathers for Liliana tonight. It made Liliana feel all shivery to realize that.

Roz turned so she was leaning against the arm of the couch, putting her feet up. There was still plenty of room for Liliana to lie down at her feet. Liliana didn't think she'd ever seen such a big couch before. She took off her own boots, and socks, and lay down, her head almost touching Roz's feet, but not quite.

Huh. This was weird. Roz felt far away, even though her feet were so close. Liliana's heart started going fast, she wasn't even sure why, except she felt alone and being alone right in this moment hurt, and was scary. She wrapped her arms around herself and started to rock. She was surprised to hear Roz speaking to her. She actually jumped.

"No, this isn't right. You're too far away."

Liliana sat up and looked at her. Roz gestured, saying, "You need to be closer." Roz removed the cushions on the back of the couch, tugged up her skirt so she could spread her legs, and patted the space between her thighs. "Here. This is where you should be. Come lay your head on my thigh, girl. Don't worry about mussing my dress, I wouldn't mind that at all."

Oh. That was not far away, at all. Liliana couldn't imagine being much closer than that, really. She scooted up the couch, not particularly gracefully but she got there, and laid her head on Roz's wide muscular thigh, reminding herself it was okay if her makeup got on it, Roz had said so. Roz pressed her foot into Liliana's big belly. That felt good. Like cuddling, or maybe like being hugged by Roz's legs. Liliana took a breath, let herself go a bit. This couch, this woman, could hold her weight.

Roz was working Liliana's hair out of its ponytail and it ached a bit 'cause she'd had it up since the morning. Then Roz's hands were in it, her fingers dragging through it, and it was all this sensation at once. So much, so close, Liliana was shivering again, and her feet were twitching.

"Yes, girl. This is better. I want you close so I can touch you."

Oh my. It had been so long since anyone had touched her except Violet. It felt . . . surprising that Roz would want to. She was breathing kind of raggedly now, just trying to accept that Roz wanted to touch her.

"Your hair is a pleasure, girl. So much abundance."

Liliana just focused on breathing. This was already over-whelming. Her feet were full-on fluttering now.

"Your hair is the key, isn't it? I can find you this way."

What did that even mean? Find her? She was right here. Roz worked her hands into Liliana's hair until she had it by the roots. Then she twisted. Ohhh. Liliana was trembling, and she was pretty sure she had just moaned. That might be the yummiest pain Liliana had ever experienced. She could feel the way it made her relax. Roz did it again, and she might have mouthed Roz's thigh through her dress. Not on purpose but damn that was divine. Her feet stopped fluttering. Oh this was good. So so good.

Liliana flowed with it, as Roz gave her pulse after pulse of that delicious pain. She was writhing between Roz's thighs soaking up every bit of it, as Roz murmured encouragements. It was glorious, and there was so much of it. It felt like it was filling her up, drop by drop, until she was smiling and sated, nuzzling Roz's gorgeously thick thigh, and Roz eased her hands out of Liliana's hair, and stroked her face.

Roz put her hand on the back of Liliana's neck, and just held it there, like it was settling in. It felt right, there, like that was of course where it should be. Like it tethered them together in exactly the way they needed.

"Girl, you are a delight," Roz said, her voice languorous.

The words fluttered over her skin, and she let them, the soft feather of them feeling okay right then. Probably because of the hand anchoring the back of her neck. Was this what being trea-sured was like? Her whole body felt like it was gleaming.

Not that she wanted to move just then. She definitely wanted to stay right there until Roz wanted her somewhere else. There was this pulse that kept happening at the place where Roz's fingertips were on Liliana's neck. It felt like building energy for ritual, but this didn't have a job to do, it just moved between them in these beautiful waves that felt like they held her so safe, like she was floating. Was Roz a witch too?

"You just sink right into submission, don't you? What a good girl you are."

Oh. Oh my. Those words weren't feathers on her skin, they were shimmers inside her chest, all gorgeous and new and bursting and it was so much, felt so big. She opened her eyes, turning her head to see Ma'am's face, to be sure she hadn't dreamed those words. Roz was smiling, as she kept her hand in exactly that spot on the back of Liliana's neck, pulsing into her.

"Yes, you heard me right. You are a good brave girl to reach for this, to let yourself have it, to let yourself shine."

That was so much to hold. Liliana tried, but it built in her chest and had nowhere to go. It just got bigger and bigger till she couldn't breathe from it and then it flowed out of her eyes, and she could finally breathe again.

"Okay, girl. I have a job for you."

Liliana smiled. A job specifically for her. It was amazing how lucky that made her feel.

"Sit up for me now."

Liliana extricated herself from Roz, and sat, waiting. She breathed it in, the waiting to hear how she could be useful. This moment was good all on its own, full of anticipation and purpose and clarity.

"You know Femme Brunch is tomorrow. I need you to iron my dress, and pick out the right accessories for it."

Oh my. Liliana's hands started fluttering and a smile burst onto her face. Yes, she wanted to do this. To do it right.

"Oh you like that, do you girl?"

"Yes, Ma'am."

"I will be wearing the black dress that's hanging by the mirror over there. There's a tabletop ironing board in that corner, that you can put on the coffee table so you can sit while you iron my dress."

The dress flowed like water in her hands, all soft and dark. She brought that over first, before fetching the ironing board and the iron. She worked carefully, at first conscious of Roz's gaze on her as she did the task. But soon she sunk into it deep, getting every bit of the dress methodically, her lip between her teeth. Until she was done. Then she smiled, because it had felt good to let herself drop into hyperfocus like that. It felt a lot like Roz's hand on her neck, actually. She reached up, and stroked her hand against the back of her neck, raising her eyes to look at Roz's face.

"Let me see."

Roz took the dress, looked it over. Nodded once in approval.

"Good. Now I need you to select a corset to go over it. There are three in my suitcase."

The first was teal, with silver butterflies on it. The second was burgundy with black lace. The last was black velvet. Liliana immediately rejected the teal one, though she was sad to do so because it matched Ma'am's nails. But it wouldn't work with a black dress underneath. The burgundy might. She chewed her lip, thinking about Roz, and the things she'd seen her wear before. No, the burgundy wasn't right either. It would cut the dress in the wrong place. She put the others away and carried the black corset over to Roz.

"This one, Ma'am."

"Yes, that will do nicely. Now I need you to pick out something to cover my arms that works with both of these. There are a few long-sleeved options in the suitcase."

Liliana sorted through them. The royal blue was too casual. The white would bunch up, she thought. Black again. Damn that would look hot, all that black lace on her bare arms. She got a smile from Roz when she brought it over.

"Pick out some jewelry from the box on the table."

She sat at the table. It had been enough walking for a bit, her knee said she needed to sit. She pulled together the picture in her mind of the corset, the dress, the lace shirt. Silver closures on the corset meant she should choose the silver ring with a royal-blue flower. Yes, that, and this bracelet would be perfect. No necklace, she thought. Let Ma'am's cleavage be the star and soak up the spotlight. Yes, these were right, probably. Maybe the ring was too much? She didn't think so, but . . . well she would see what Roz said.

She brought them over, and waited as Roz looked, and thought, and seemed to take forever contemplating her choices, before she smiled. Oh her smile was everything.

"Good job, girl. You did well."

Liliana felt warmth spread over her whole body. She had done it. She had completed her first service task, and done it well. She had pleased Ma'am.

"Okay, girl, lay those out on the chair and come sit next to me. I need you to massage my hands and wrists."

Liliana could think of nothing she would rather do.

YIN AND YANG

Mags Hayward

With graceful elegance she carves a path across the stage, twirling through the slithers of light that perforate the gloom. She flirts with the beams, lingering in their brilliance long enough to tease. Her face, fleetingly captured in the glare, offers a snapshot of demure beauty. Dark lashes flutter over steel-blue eyes, there's a whisper of a smile, then she's gone . . . spiraling away, chased by shadows that swirl in kaleidoscope patterns with her, the jewel at the center.

Everyone's spellbound. Fellow students crane their necks, mesmerized by her fluidity of movement. Engrossed, they scarcely breathe as she dances without music, her only accompaniment the soft tapping of pointe shoes and the metronome rhythm of collectively pounding hearts.

Natalie. A more alluring creature never lived and I can't stop looking at her. Her lithe limbs, wrapped in a flesh-toned body stocking, appear naked, exposed. Her perky breasts jiggle as she twists and turns and, from where I'm sitting, I can see every detail of her exquisite body. All of it. As she lifts her leg in a high arabesque, I gaze longingly at the puffy outline of her labia and the indent where the thin Lycra fabric stretches across her sex.

A fluttering of twinges stirs my loins and I recall the many times that svelte body has lain in my bed, thighs spread, slender fingers beckoning. I quiver at the memory of soft moans rumbling in her throat when the tip of my tongue tastes the honey beading at the mouth of her soaking slit.

I watch her twist, turn, floating toward center stage where she performs a slow, controlled, double pirouette.

Oh Natalie.

I break free of my trance. I can't afford to daydream. I have a job to do. I'm the lighting designer for Natalie's dance and the light must be honed to complement her sensuous performance.

"It's all about the movement, keep it simple."

Her whispered instructions still scorch my ear and, focusing, I subtly raise the levels, adding texture to the hazy void she dances within.

All about the movement? No, it's all about *her*. Her flawless execution of contemporary ballet surpasses anything I've seen and, for a second-year degree student, her choreography excels. Everyone is floored by her and rightly so. But to me, she's so much more than a gifted dancer. She's my world.

We're opposites, Natalie and I: light and shadow, yin and yang. While she's outgoing and confident, a natural performer, I lurk backstage away from the spotlight. Yet, together, we're a formidable pair: dancer and technician joining forces to produce the perfect, polished performance.

We enhance each other. And so it is at home. It's said opposites attract, and our relationship supports that theory. On the surface, we have nothing in common, yet we fit together like the pieces of a puzzle. Fate threw us together, or so I think. We're meant to be. I knew that from the first hello; I was drawn to her and she, to me.

Nonetheless, two years on, I still pinch myself each time she snuggles in my arms. Why has fortune favored me? I was never a lucky child, and relationships before Natalie slipped through my fingers like the beams of light I now direct. I never dreamed I'd be this happy or feel so complete.

From onstage, Natalie seeks me out. Finding me, she flashes a smile that leaves me breathless. She's so beautiful, dazzling, and all I can think about is her—touching her, kissing her, breathing in her scent. . . . My concentration wavers again and, in my reverie, I fail to notice any more of her dance.

Applause echoes around the studio and Natalie curtsies to her audience.

Oh, hell.

A cold sweat dampens my brow at the realization that I've messed up.

"Hold it there, Nat, don't move," I call out.

Turning to my lighting desk, I quickly plot a fade-out. The light dims slowly, swallowing my lover until she disappears from view. Hurriedly tapping more keys, I activate a calls state and light floods the stage. But it's overly bright, my efforts too little, too late. The magic's spoiled.

"Okay people, that's the last dance," hollers the petite, gray-haired dance mistress from her pew beside me. "Good work everyone, you're free to go. Warm-up onstage at six. Prompt." A wrinkled hand pats my shoulder. "Let's run through Natalie's piece again. I want something special."

"I'm sorry," I say. "I got distracted."

"Didn't we all? Oh, speak of the devil," she says, looking beyond me.

"Coffee or tea?"

Natalie's beside me, her soft, silky voice purring in my ear. Sweat glistens like diamonds on her olive skin and a whiff of lavender along with the bitter tang of sweat tickles my nostrils. Both scents arouse. They bring to mind late-night lovemaking among clammy, twisted sheets.

Bending low, she kisses me, parting her lips, and I taste the minty wetness of her mouth.

"Coffee," I murmur when she breaks away. "But I'm not quite done."

"Oh? Don't you want to spend time with me?"

Silly question. "I need to work on your performance piece. It's not finished."

"Didn't you make me look fabulous?"

She flutters her false lashes, heavy stage makeup creasing at the corners of her eyes. Reaching out, I brush an errant ringlet away from her face.

"I haven't done you justice. Couldn't concentrate."

"Why?" Her lips curve into a half smile and she caresses my cheek with the back of her hand. "I'll see you in the coffee bar when you're done."

She kisses my forehead and backs away.

I shudder, breath catching in my throat. With the ghost of that earlier kiss still burning on my lips, I resume my work. I summon concentration; I need to crack on. My part in Natalie's performance has to be flawless and this is my only chance to get it right, to make her shine the way she deserves. Time's precious—tonight is opening night.

I work quickly, adjusting the timings, tweaking the color. Another dancer takes to the stage, marking Natalie's movements, but I see *her*—her body, her face, her smile. I visualise her so clearly and, with that image floating before my eyes, I paint the stage around her. Satisfied, I save my work and turn to the dance mistress. Her nod of approval says I'm free to go.

Great!

Clicking on the working light, I hastily tidy away my notes before charging down the seating bank, steel-toed Doc Martens clanking. I still have preshow tasks to complete, but they can wait. I need to see Natalie. I want to hold her, kiss her, and reassure her before she takes to the stage in front of a sell-out audience. She may be confident, but she's not superhuman—preshow jitters will shake her as much as me.

I sprint toward the cafe in the theater's lobby, where Natalie's waiting. Showered and changed, she'll smell of lavender shower gel and look like an angel. *My* angel.

The cafe's packed but I soon spot Natalie. Face scrubbed of makeup, she's wearing a baggy purple sweatshirt, black leggings, and the knee-high leather boots I bought for her birthday. She's stunningly beautiful. With her dark brows, long lashes, and hair still twisted into an intricate bun, she has the look of a young Audrey Hepburn, even in casual clothing. It's her poise, her mannerisms, and that enchanting smile.

Noticing me, she holds two Styrofoam cups aloft and gestures toward the exit.

"Upstairs," she mouths.

Good idea. There's a bar on the second floor that won't be open to the public for another hour. It's probably locked but I have a key. Skirting around the cafe, I head for the stairs while Natalie squeezes through the melee, her slender frame slotting through impossibly narrow gaps. She smiles and comments as she passes friends. Cheeks are kissed and shoulders touched in flirtatious gestures.

I don't mind. When she reaches me, I'll be greeted with a warm hug and a kiss full-on the lips. Only I get that. *Oops* . . . I hop over a bag dumped haphazardly in my path, its contents spilling from the open top. I smile; dancers can be so untidy. My dancer is.

And here she comes.

My smile widens as we close the gap between us.

"Hey there, gorgeous."

Natalie slides her arms around my waist, her cheek brushing mine before her lips press down on my mouth. She lets the kiss linger before nuzzling my neck.

"How are you holding up?" she whispers. "Did you fix the lighting?"

"Yes, and I'm fine." I kiss the top of her head, tasting hairspray. "You?"

"Good. I'm good."

"Honestly?"

She looks up. "I'm a little nervous. But that's a good thing. No point dancing if it doesn't excite." She shrugs. "Did I do okay?"

"Oh yes." I cup her face in my hands. "You stole the show."

"I doubt that." Natalie laughs. "But thank you. Upstairs?"

"Uh-huh."

"Oh . . . your coffee." She hands me one of the Styrofoam cups. "Almost forgot. Almost spilled it on you, too," she adds, grinning. "Come on."

Her delicate hand slips into mine, the warmth of her grip promising more kisses and cuddling, perhaps a little petting. Lewd images invade my brain, visions of intimate acts performed on the soft, leather sofas in the closed bar. *I wish* . . .

Natalie walks a step ahead of me, pert ass waggling inside her tight leggings. My gaze is drawn to those jostling cheeks and I notice the lack of panty line. Naughty girl. No knickers. Her breasts aren't restrained either. They tremble teasingly within her sweatshirt, begging to be fondled and sucked.

I float up the staircase, following Natalie's snaking wiggle as if hypnotized. I love her ass; I adore her figure and the sassy way she moves. At home, she complains about being too thin and calls herself an "ungainly stick-insect." True, she is slender, but with all the exercise she does, it's hardly surprising. But *ungainly?* Certainly not. Everything about her is elegant. My little "stick-insect" is perfect and, *ooh*, she's sexy.

Reaching the first-floor bar, Natalie tries the door. It isn't locked but the lights are off and the metal shutters are secured across the serving area.

"Shall we?" she asks.

Cautious, I peep inside. Deserted. The evening sunlight streams through the floor-to-ceiling windows, illuminating every corner of the room in brilliant golden tones and casting shadows across the empty sofas and chairs. Any movement would be apparent.

"This way."

Natalie leads me to the far end of the room where unexpected intruders won't disturb us. There, she takes my coffee cup and deposits it with hers on a low table.

"Just you and me," she says, burrowing against me.

Yes . . . you and me.

I love these stolen moments. I live for them. Snippets of time alone with Natalie, slotted between the chaos of rehearsals, performances, endless deadlines—for both of us. Quiet moments where time draws a breath.

Sighing, Natalie flops onto a sofa and pats the cushion beside her. When I sit, she encircles me in her arms and we melt into each other, becoming one as we kiss, slow and deep, lips parted. I taste her, feel her, I am as one with her. Moaning softly, she pulls away. She smiles, a crooked, impish smile, then yanks her sweatshirt over her head, revealing a skimpy vest beneath.

"Nat," I glance around nervously, "what're you doing?"

"Relax, no one can see us." Her nipples poke at the thin material. Stroking them, pinching them, she teases me. "Do you want these? Do they turn you on?"

Turn me on? My sex burns with a throbbing, needy yearning

but I'm not as brave as Natalie. Intimacy outside the bedroom bothers me. I hesitate, but she gazes at me with doe eyes and I can't resist her. I never can. Sighing helplessly, I ease her vest aside and gently draw a nipple into my mouth.

Oh yes . . .

The uneven texture, the salty taste, sends my pulse racing. I switch to the other breast, not wanting to neglect it.

Craving more, I raise Natalie's arms, hook the vest over her head, and gently guide her backward onto the padded leather. Her dark nipples stand proud, inviting me to touch them. With trembling fingertips, I lightly circle the hardened bumps. Slowly, I spiral outward, gently massaging her areolae and the fleshy mounds they crown.

Touching her is exciting, arousing, and I gasp when a delicious twinge tickles my pussy. Lifting my hands from her flesh, I take a moment to gaze upon my gorgeous partner.

"Um . . . don't stop."

Natalie's eyelids flutter and a strand of hair escapes from her bun, springing into a kiss curl above the center of her forehead.

"Do that again, and take this off." She tugs at my sweater. "I want some boob, too."

Now, there's an offer I can't refuse.

My nipples ache at the mere thought of Natalie's hands upon my breasts or her tongue swirling over my aroused buds. I scan the room, peering into every corner, but all is quiet. I remove my sweater and T-shirt. The bra I'm wearing is practical, not pretty, but it cups my large breasts in a way that enhances my cleavage.

"That's more like it," Natalie says, smirking. "Hello, beauties."

She finds my breasts irresistible and, sure enough, her gaze zooms in on my wobbling flesh. A flush blooms across my skin, fueled by desire and the longing to be fondled . . . but I'm not bold enough to remove the bra.

What if we're disturbed?

Still covered, I turn my attention to Natalie. She's got me fired up and my pussy pulsates under her lustful looks and wandering hands. No longer content to fondle gently, I dive on her, lavishing her with kisses from her breasts to her neck—hard, passionate kisses that leave her flesh goose-bumped and trembling.

I stroke her breasts, kneading them in my palms before moving down to her flat stomach. Gazing into her eyes, I slide a hand beneath the elastic waist of her leggings. Natalie squirms beneath me, hips gently grinding. Her sharp gasp shatters the quietness when my fingertips make contact with her sensitive folds. She's soaking, dripping, and my fingers soon become slick with her juices.

I stroke her clit, then rub harder, faster, my little circles making Natalie groan louder. I flick her engorged nub, then plunge two fingers deep inside her sex. They emerge drenched and, feeling devilish, I lick them clean.

"Do I taste good?"

There's a wicked smirk on Natalie's face and, *ooh, yes*, she's sweet as honey. She always is. I've never tasted a woman as mouth-watering.

"You're scrumptious," I say.

I suddenly get the urge to pull off her boots, peel down her leggings, and bury my face in her smooth, shaved snatch. I want to eat her, lap up every drop of her sticky nectar . . . but I can't. Not here. The bar staff may arrive at any moment.

"Fuck me, please, fuck me," Natalie urges, reading my thoughts. "Please, I want you."

I want her too, I really do. I watch her writhing, sighing, craving my touch . . .

Oh, what the hell? Screw getting caught!

I kiss her lips and probe her slick depths, sliding my fingers deep inside. She's warm, wet. I smell the musky tang of her arousal. I need to make love to my Natalie.

I drive my fingers into her, fast and hard, making her moan and arch her back. I thrust again. And again. I know how to please her, know exactly what she likes—the right depth, pace, pressure—to send her hurtling toward a quick, satisfying climax. Bent over, watching her, I fuck her with my fingers and my darling girl bucks her hips to meet my thrusts. Loud groans escape her throat and her soft depths clench my fingers.

"Ooh . . . Yes . . . "

Natalie's body stiffens, then jolts as an orgasm rips through her. She pants and whimpers while spasms shake her body. As the waves subside, she exhales slowly, her eyelids flutter, and the most delightful smile illuminates her face.

"You're so good," she murmurs.

Grasping my wrists, she gently withdraws my fingers and guides them into her mouth. She sucks them clean.

"Mmm." She smiles. "I do taste yummy."

Puckering her lips, she kisses me. The kiss becomes increasingly passionate and I find myself being pushed backward onto the soft sofa. Natalie climbs on top of me, switching roles. She reaches around to unclasp my bra, removing it before I can protest. She sucks a hard nipple into her mouth and rolls the other between her fingertips. Breathless with bliss, I gasp for air.

Suddenly, she goes for the zip of my jeans.

"Natalie, no!"

My mind fills with images of gawping bar staff and scandalized members of the public.

"Shush," she says, touching my lips. "Let me love you."

"But Nat . . . "

It's no use, she's adamant. And anyway, my modesty's rapidly overcome by lustful desire. I want her. I need to feel her tongue upon me. I must have my release.

Putty in her hands, I allow Natalie to unzip my jeans and

yank them down. They won't go past my ankles, not with my boots on, so I'm left shackled. Exposed and effectively bound, I'm completely at Natalie's mercy and the impish glint in her eyes tells me she loves that. Moaning softly, almost purring, she rolls off the sofa and crawls stealthily between my thighs, gently parting them. My anticipation builds as she tugs aside my thong.

My pulse is racing. I'm fit to burst. I gasp when, suddenly, her hot, wet tongue laps the length of my slit. It feels so good, so *fucking* good, sending delicious shivers racing through my body. Another lick creates a prolonged quiver and my hips move uncontrollably, as if bewitched.

Natalie grasps my thighs and fucks me with her tongue. I feel it inside me, the warmth, the movement. I'm delirious with pleasure. My hips undulate to the steady rhythm of Natalie's thrusts, like a dance; a horny, needy dance with an ever-increasing tempo. I love it. I love every moment.

My head falls back, my arms are limp. In a change of tack, she seals her lips around my clit and sucks—*hard*. That's it, I'm gone. Already approaching climax, my body gives in.

"Oh fuck, Natalie. Fuck, fuck, *fuck!*"

I jolt, squirm, pussy muscles contracting in powerful waves while she laps, kitten-like, sucking up the juices that stream from my depths. And when the waves pass, she crawls onto my lap, curling against me.

We lie in silence, holding each other while we come down. It's a perfect moment. Quiet. Still. Another snippet of time captured in a bubble to treasure for a lifetime. But time doesn't hold its breath forever.

"I have to go. So do you." I sigh. "Come on, we've got a show to do."

"Already?"

Groaning, Natalie slides from the sofa and slowly uncurls. Glancing at her watch, she gasps.

"Oh my . . . I have to go. The warm-up starts in five minutes and I need to change."

She hastily gathers her clothing and dresses standing, apparently not caring if she's seen. It's not so for me: aware of my surroundings again, I find my scattered clothes on hand and knees and nervously pull them on.

Dressed, Natalie points to the crotch of her leggings.

"Look what you've done," she says, with a look of mock horror.

Grinning, I shrug. "Well, if you will insist on going without knickers."

My sweet angel giggles, laughter lines creasing her face, but her gaze returns to her watch and her smile fades.

"Hell. I'm late."

"Hey Nat," I say, anticipating a swift exit. I trail my hand down her arm, stroking her downy hairs. "Good luck."

"Aw, thank you." She kisses my forehead. "Good luck to you, too. Make me look ethereal."

As if she could look anything else.

"I'll see you after the show." Blowing a kiss, Natalie backs away. "I love you."

My heart lurches. It does every time I hear her say those words.

"I love you, too."

She beams at me, a beautiful, wide smile, then turns and scurries across the room. She hauls open the door, charges through, and clatters down the stairs. The door swings shut and silence envelops the room.

I draw a breath. It may be a peaceful, quiet bar but I know it won't be for long. And I still have work to do. Time to move. I straighten my clothes and sit up. Natalie will deliver a stunning performance but she needs my contribution to make her shine. All set to go, I waver.

One more minute, to savor the moment.

Resting my head on the sofa back, I pick up my lukewarm coffee and slurp. I lick my lips, tasting Natalie and coffee. A smile dimples my cheeks and I shake my head.

Ah, Natalie.

I can't believe how lucky I am.

STILL MARCHING

Victoria Janssen

Rhiannon Farnon licked trail mix crumbs from her palm. She struggled to get her glove back on, cursing and juggling her over-sized poster in the brisk January wind. The sign read, I CAN'T BELIEVE I STILL HAVE TO PROTEST THIS SHIT.

An inspiring speech boomed from a nearby amplifier on the Ben Franklin Parkway, but she had lost track of which city coun-cilperson was up, and was so far away from the stage that she couldn't make out most of the words.

"Ma'am?"

When had she become a *ma'am*? Giving her motorcycle glove one last yank, Rhiannon turned to the young woman who was, unsurprisingly, wearing a vivid magenta pussy hat. "Yes?"

"Is it okay if I take your picture? Both of you have the same poster."

Rhiannon glanced to her left, noting the duplicate sign actually read I CAN'T FUCKING BELIEVE I'VE STILL GOT TO PROTEST THIS BULLSHIT. Close enough. Then she looked up from the dark-skinned hands holding the profane version of her sign and gaped. "Mavis?"

Mavis Jackson grinned, sideways and sly. "Hey lady. Long time no see." She threw her arm over Rhiannon's shoulders, lifting her sign at a jaunty angle. Stunned, Rhiannon did the same, for one breathless moment unable to look away from Mavis's perfect profile, and the one distaff earring dangling from her right earlobe.

The camera clicked rapidly. As the photographer smiled her thanks and faded into the crowd, Rhiannon forgot about her completely, dropping her sign to seize Mavis's shoulders. "What the hell are you doing in Philly? Where have you been?"

Mavis tossed her sign onto the grass, leaned in, and grabbed Rhiannon around the waist, squeezing hard. Bemused, Rhiannon hugged back, her eyes welling with tears. "It's great to see you," she said.

Mavis smelled like cocoa butter, a visceral reminder of when they'd met, over twenty-five years ago in DC, at a huge march for abortion rights. Mavis, wearing a leather bikini top, had inscribed MY BODY, MY CHOICE in white paint on her bare back and stomach. Rhiannon had been carrying giant bundles of sage gifted to her by her mother and aunts from the coven, smudging away as she walked, alternating chants with nightmarish screams, her long broomstick skirt dangling with wire hangers and streaked with fake blood. They'd met because another marcher needed a tampon; Rhiannon always had supplies with her, and Mavis had been wearing several as part of a crown atop her brunette curls. And then . . . well. The back of the bus Mavis's college had sent had been cramped but private. Rhiannon had ridden back with them, the beginning of the most intense weeks of her life.

Mavis's hair, now worn in chin-length dreadlocks, was streaked with gray; Rhiannon's, cut to bristle a decade before, had gone white early. Mavis stepped back and stroked Rhiannon's cheek. "Holy shit, lady. Nobody heard anything from you after you went out West."

Rhiannon's cheeks flamed. She cast her eyes down at Mavis's T-shirt, which read, succinctly, EMOLUMENTS! "Oh. Yeah. I, umm, I went out there with some, well, bikers."

"*Bikers?!*"

"Lesbian bikers! Not, like, the Pagans. I mean, they *were* pagans, some of them knew my aunties—"

Mavis was doubled over laughing now, hands on her knees as she whooped and gasped for air. After a moment or two, Rhiannon was laughing, too, at the very thought of them, two middle-aged women in the middle of a massive Women's March, overcome by a reunion that had taken far too long.

The speeches, as she'd predicted, ran late. Slowly, Rhiannon and Mavis drifted ahead of the remaining marchers, where folding chairs had been set up in front of the stage. In the front row, Rhiannon leaned against Mavis's strong shoulder while her old lover videoed impassioned speeches on her phone.

Later in the afternoon, after most of the marchers had wandered home to their lives, there was a final rousing song Rhiannon didn't know, and the speaker was encouraging everyone to take their trash with them. Mavis offered Rhiannon the last of the water in her red bottle. Rhiannon swigged it gratefully and handed it back. Their eyes met and held. Time contracted.

Mavis's eyes, gorgeous translucent brown and gold, shimmered now with the beginnings of tears. "Rhi," she said, "I didn't have a lot of hope when I showed up for this thing today, but now . . . ." She looked down, ostensibly to stuff her water bottle into her sleek leather messenger bag.

Rhiannon dug in her jeans pocket for a tissue. "I was thinking more like, 'at least we'll have each other for the apocalypse.'"

Mavis snorted and ran her hand over the top of Rhiannon's crew cut. "You are still the most cynical Witch I've ever met."

"My moms and aunts are a lot bitchier these days, too," Rhiannon said. "So—why Philly?"

"Know how I said I was joining the radical separatists, and my granny had other ideas?"

"Yeah?" They joined the stream of marchers leaving the parkway.

"I went to law school."

Rhiannon grinned hugely. "I bet she loved that."

"She does! She lives in Orlando now. But anyway, I just took a job in Philly, with the DA's office. Started first of the year. It's mostly outreach, recruitment—get some People of Color into the power structure."

"You're going to make changes, real changes. Probably without even getting punched in the face. You sure you're okay with that?"

"I've come to terms with it," Mavis said breezily. "And you?"

"I still have a bike," Rhiannon said, "but now I teach math. Little kids, in West Philly. I have a big old house on Osage all to myself and my cats. Plenty of room, if you ever want to slide by."

"I bought a condo," Mavis said, then caught Rhiannon as she pretended to faint. "I didn't have a lot of transition time, and I'm not locked into it for another six months—quit laughing at me! It's right on the parkway, you could come use my nice clean bathroom right this minute!"

"Done!" Rhiannon said, happily.

And so Rhiannon found herself looking out a twentieth-floor window, down Philadelphia's answer to the Champs-Élysées, while Mavis made coffee in the open-plan kitchen. The extent of her decorating was an open suitcase just inside the bedroom door, a stack of law journals on the living room carpet, and a bright red puffer coat, dropped on a folding chair near the door. Their discarded signs lay on the blandly neutral carpet, beneath Rhiannon's motorcycle jacket and rainbow-striped scarf.

She'd gone to the march out of duty, her heart and her feet heavy with thoughts of a world in even worse shape than the year before, her gut twisted with fear for the future of her classrooms full of kids. But right now . . . she drew in a deep breath, smelling rich fresh coffee, centering herself here, in this moment.

"I swear I'm getting furniture," Mavis said. "Just haven't had time." She set their mugs on the floor, atop journals, before joining Rhiannon on the floor.

"I have furniture at my place, not just cats," Rhiannon said. "You are welcome any time. For as long as you want."

"I—really? I mean, it's been like twenty-five years. Are you sure?"

Rhiannon studied Mavis's face. "I've had twenty-five years to think about it. And to regret that I didn't follow you."

"I . . . I couldn't have stayed. But I wanted to. I really wanted to."

Rhiannon lifted her coffee mug and they toasted. "To hope, for a pair of cranky middle-aged ladies. We've done all right for ourselves, after all."

"To living in the midst of apocalypse, together," Mavis said, and they clinked mugs again. They drank. After a long, silent interval, she said, "I don't have a couch, but I do have a bed. You're invited to visit me there."

Rhiannon smiled. "I am happy to accept your invitation."

Mavis's bedroom was still sparse, holding only a lamp and her suitcase in addition to the big bed. "I bought a new mattress," she said, with a shy smile, as she slowly unbuttoned Rhiannon's plaid shirt. "The first I ever paid for myself. At my age."

"I only bought my house five years ago," Rhiannon admitted. "After I finally split with Marina."

"Come to think of it I did hear a few things through the

grapevine. She's still in New York?" Mavis pushed the shirt from Rhiannon's shoulders, followed by her bra straps.

"Yeah . . . " Rhiannon caught Mavis's face between her hands and kissed her, kept kissing her as Mavis unhooked her bra, and unbuttoned her jeans, caressing her ass and thighs as she pushed them down her legs to the floor.

Then Mavis knelt on the carpet, embracing Rhiannon's hips. "I still fucking love giving head," she noted.

"I seem to recall you were pretty good at it," Rhiannon said. "If I'm remembering right."

Mavis caressed her ass and nuzzled until Rhiannon shifted her feet farther apart. "Well, let's see if I can remember how to do this. . . ."

Sometime later, as they lay side by side on the mattress, Rhiannon murmured, "I want to finish undressing you now. May I do that? Then I want to get you off."

In answer, Mavis took Rhiannon's hands between hers and placed them at the waistband of her jeans. Rhiannon summoned the energy to sit up and crouched above her, tugging the jeans down and off her feet, taking the time to remove her fuzzy socks as well. "These are cute," she noted, sleepily. "You do cute now?"

"I do if they're also warm," Mavis said.

"I got over the thing with dildos," Rhiannon remarked. "Did I tell you?"

Mavis giggled. "That did not come up in conversation yet. They're no longer tools of the patriarchy?"

"It was *On Our Backs* in the nineties that did it for me," Rhiannon said, tossing the jeans and socks onto the pile decorating the bare carpet. "I didn't bring one with me to the march, though."

"I don't carry one everywhere, either." Rhiannon gave her a look. "Not any more, anyway. My toys are still in Chicago, with the rest of my stuff."

"We'll make do," Rhiannon said, lowering herself into Mavis' waiting arms and chewing delicately on her earlobe, to distract temporarily from the finger teasing her labia.

Mavis gasped and pushed into Rhiannon's hand. "There's a vibe in the suitcase, though."

"Mmm?"

Mavis hooked her knee over Rhiannon's shoulder, grasping fitfully at her arm. "There, right there, hold it there—"

The vibrator was a wand type that plugged in, right next to the bed. No worries about the batteries going out. Rhiannon circled the soft head gently where Mavis gasped the loudest, while watching her eyelids flutter, her mouth twist in pleasure. "You're so beautiful. I feel like I've never seen you before today."

Mavis didn't reply, busy shuddering through another orgasm. Rhiannon lifted the vibe away when Mavis flapped her hand in its general direction, then lay down to cuddle with her in the sweaty sheets. Her breathing slowed and steadied. Rhiannon snuggled closer. She murmured, "You know what? I am not going on the Internet for the rest of the weekend."

Mavis huffed out a laugh. "Big words, lady."

"Do you want to come to my place later on?"

"Yeah." Mavis tipped their foreheads together. "I want to see what kind of home you made. I always thought you would be good at that." She paused. "Not like in the patriarchal way, you understand."

"I do. I have three spare sets of sheets, all of them clean. And some dildos."

"And cats," Mavis reminded her, around a yawn. "Should I bring a moving van?"

"If you want." Rhiannon stroked her hand down Mavis's side.

"I just don't want us to wander off and do our own thing for another twenty-five years."

"Me neither. I think . . . I want to see how things turn out if we both stick around."

"Like glue. Hey, I'll take you for a sexy ride on my lesbian motorcycle."

"We'll go yell at all the protest marches. Together."

"Next time, we're not having matching signs, though."

"We'll make them together, just to be sure."

SWEET OF MY HEART

Anna Watson

Charmed Soul, Sweet. 1931, New York City
I have never vibrated. I look upon Father's sweet little face, I look
upon His sweet little body, and I know He is God. I know this in
every part of myself, but I do not vibrate like the other Sweets.
Oh, I envy them. I yearn to join with them as they make their
noises and move their bodies in hitches and starts and look almost
as if they are taking fits, but it is the glory of God filling their
bodies. The most pure expression of our love of God! Oh, it is
ecstasy they show when they vibrate! How I wish to join them! I
have failed, and must try harder.

Mimi LaRouge, Dance Hall Girl
When I first heard about the free meals given out by Father Divine's
Peace Mission, I was too worried about using up my shoe leather
to walk there. If the bosses see you have holes or breaks in your
shoes, they will give you a warning, and then another. But then it
got to where I was just too hungry and I thought if I fainted from
being so famished one evening, fainted right when I was dancing

with some joe, wouldn't that be worse than another layer of sole gone in the walk to Harlem?

Charmed Soul
We Sweets sit at the table with Father as He makes His rounds. Every Peace Mission banquet we visit, we see the beautiful work of God: hungry people finding solace in our good, honest food with no difference made between the light complected and the dark complected, for we are all equal, all worthy. My so-called mother thought I would come to ruin, but here I am, doing God's work. I sit at the table and I can see God. I eat with God. "I raised you to be a lady!" my so-called mother would say. "To be nice and dainty! And look at you, ugly, gawky, clumping around like a common laborer!" I labor for God now, and He looks upon me with love.

Mimi LaRouge
When I got to that first banquet, there was a line reaching all around the block. Tidily dressed devotees, both white and Negro, ushered us along, saying, "Peace!" and "Welcome!" and "Come inside and eat!" I could smell the cooking, we all could, and I knew I had made the right decision, even though I could feel the scratch of the sidewalk through my soles.

Inside was clean and crowded, but we were moved right along. I was seated at a table between a Negro man who seemed to shrink away from me and a Negro grandmother, also shy. Across the table was another white girl, who stuck out her grubby hand and gave mine a shake. Her name was Nancy and she was only fifteen. She asked me if I knew God. Now, I've gotten in trouble before by saying the truth, that I am agnostic, so I just smiled. Nancy laughed out loud.

"I knew it!" she said, patting my hand. "I could see your goodness, I could see it shining out of your eyes! Shall I come over and tell you a secret?" She skipped around the table and put her lips to my ear. Up close, I could smell that she was unwashed, well, many of us are and thank goodness for the *eau de cologne Maman* left with me. "Keep coming back and one day, you will see God in this very banquet hall!" She would have said more, but just then the food was served, oh, chicken fricassee, oh, liver and onions, oh, creamed peas! Oh, tapioca pudding and angel food cake! *Sacré bleu*, I ate until I felt ill!

Charmed Soul
Dear Daughter tells us that Father will visit retribution on the newspaper journalist who cast aspersions on His holy name. "Flood, fires, broken limbs! Death!" She flings up her arms and looks to the sky and we all say with her, "Wonderful, wonderful, wonderful!" We sing, "Let them come in 'dust and ashes,' Let them moan and seek GOD's Face; Let them feel the bitter lashes, And of their own evil get just a taste." I know that Father can do these things. A woman came into our heaven and she said to our faces that she was virginal, snow white, as we must all be, but Holy Light Shines saw her duck down an alley with a man. Father cast her out and visited retribution on her for her falsehoods, and that woman began to take fits. She took so many fits that she shook herself right to death. That woman was destroyed by the wrath of Father. I must work harder.

Mimi LaRouge
I tie some rags around my shoes for the daily walk to Harlem, and take them off when I get to the banquet. Behind our chairs, the Divinites, who are called "angels," sing and clap, joyful voices raised, and it is a joy surely echoed in my belly. I am beginning to have a bit more flesh on my body, and the men at the dance hall like that. They like a girl whose figure is filled out. At night,

I dream of braised rabbit and mashed potatoes. There is even gravy! I've tried to get the other girls to go, especially Sue, as she is so slight to begin with, but she is vehement that she will not sit with a Negro, not even if she were starving! It is a flaw and a mistake for her to say so. *Maman* saw Josephine Baker dance and *Maman* herself danced the night through to music from the Negro jazz musicians, all of this in *le gai Paris*, before she met Daddy and he moved her here to America, to our farm in Vermont. *Maman* would never let me grow up with such narrow views about humanity as Sue holds.

I had nearly forgotten what Nancy told me that first day, but then one time, sure enough, I reached the banquet and there was a tremendous excitement and to-do. The angels bustled and ordered us around and then there was a great shouting and singing and here came a little Negro man in such important, fancy clothes, and on his head, there was a beautiful gray fedora and around him, adoring, a phalanx of ladies. Nancy was suddenly at my side, leaning against me, interpreting.

"Look there, you see the lady angels come in with Father? They are called his Sweets, they are his very special secretaries." Some of the Sweets were pretty, some were young, some were older than *Maman* and very homely. One was what some might call mannish and what I call strong and calm, collected and capable, like a thoroughbred. A fine specimen. I watched her march to her place at God's table. I had heard enough from Nancy and others by now to know that the angels and these Sweets truly believed this man was God. How *Maman* would have screamed with laughter! How Sue would screw up her face in disgust! Nancy bounced up and down, her dirty face wreathed with smiles.

"What do you think, oh, what do you think? He is truly God, do you not believe it as well?" She gripped my arm and shook it. I smiled and pulled away. I couldn't answer her as she would have liked, but I had by now learned more about this Peace Mission. Both Negroes and white followers of Father Divine cook and serve the meals and no one is turned away. Diners are seated white next to Negro; it is a rule called "enacting the bill," by which they mean The Bill of Rights. So although I do not believe little Father is Divine, I like his menu, and I approve of this work putting forward the equality of all men.

Charmed Soul
I praise, praise, praise Father! How good He is, to feed all these poor souls! I joyfully accompany the other Sweets to Harlem, coming to the city from our country heaven, where I work and where I first found God. There is a girl. I do not know her name. I see her take rags from her feet before she enters our heaven, I see how she has a good and hearty appetite and I like to see her tucking in. Some light-complected people like myself are wary and distrustful of dark-complected people, but this girl sparkles and is kind with those around her, no matter their complexions. I have seen her talking to an old, dark-complected woman, and pat her shoulder and offer her comfort. She has served from the pot to a little dark-complected child, and laughed, and said the child was "a dear little thing" and said to the child's mother, "What a pretty daughter you have!" She herself is very pretty. We have some pretty girls in the Sweets, though it is a sin for me to notice, but none as pretty as this girl. I am not sorry that Psalms of Praise has been removed from her duty, and I have been put in charge of this heaven's banquet instead, although it means moving from the country. It is not right to say that I miss the cool evenings out-of-doors when I can watch the moon rise if I am not working, but I am flawed and I think it anyway. I am flawed, and I think, "At least I may see the pretty girl."

Mimi LaRouge

Maman assures me there are many girls such as I have proven to be. She knew some in Paris, she says, and they were good, fine people. "But you will be luckier in love in a big city, *chérie*," she told me, and that has certainly proven to be true. There have certainly been a few girls who made my heart flutter, but none of them have had such an effect as the girl at the Peace Mission banquet. There are other heavens within walking distance, but I return again and again to the first place where I met my little friend, Nancy, and where my fine specimen is the Sweet in charge. It is a pleasure to watch how skillfully she manages every aspect of the banquet, how she makes things run so smoothly. And she is so handsome! She is clearly indifferent to making any feminine efforts with appearance, although she is as clean and neat as any of Father Divine's angels. Her strawberry blonde hair is gathered in one long braid, keeping it out of her honest, freckled face. Her lips are somewhat thin, but slightly curved up in a private smile much of the time. All the same, her hazel eyes with their long lashes strike me as harboring some secret worry.

As for myself, with the money I'm saving on meals, I can afford to bathe regularly now, and I keep the *eau de cologne* for when I go to the banquet and I know I will see my crush. I know her name now, too, a strange one, as all the angels have. It is Charmed Soul, but to myself, I call her Charlie.

Charmed Soul

Father is here today, blessing us with His presence, eating with us at this banquet and now, it has begun! We are singing "Just to Look at You" and first it is Beatific Garden who leaves off singing and shouts, "God! God! God!" her face shining, her limbs beginning to wander as she rises from her seat, pushes back the chair and spins and spins in place, still shouting out. Many Acts of Love remains seated, but her whole body trembles and goes into spasm, lifting her almost completely out of her chair. Adoring Child is crying and hollering; Smiling Every Day falls to her knees and crawls under the table where she rolls around, knocking into our feet, keening and weeping and filled with such love for God. They are so lively and radiating! They express their love so perfectly! I am filled with love, as well, but I do not vibrate. Desperately, I look up and around the banquet. So many angels filled and filled and filled, spilling and vibrating! The regulars and the newcomers who are hungry pay little attention, but my gaze catches that of the pretty girl, who has shoved her plate away and leans her elbows on the table, watching with such merry eyes. I look away quickly, but I have caught it! I have caught the joy! "God! God! God!" I shout and do not remember what follows, only that I am consumed by a great love.

Mimi LaRouge

Some agitation is growing at the table of Sweets. They have been singing one of their quirky, many-versed songs, the one about seeing his dear little feet and hands and the rest of it. The object of their worship pays no heed at all. Then, with no warning whatsoever, the Sweet to his right contracts upon herself, as if gut shot. She lets loose a great whoop and seems overcome with the fidgets. The flailing movements of her limbs propel her backward in her chair, which tips over into the singing mass of Divinites behind her. She tumbles onto the floor where I can no longer see her, but I can hear her breathy yelps. Now the effect spreads, and one after another, the Sweets careen full tilt into ecstasy. They quiver, they teeter-totter. They rise or fall from their chairs, they stagger and convulse. Across from me, Nancy begins to breathe heavily and I reach over to squeeze her hand. "Oh, see their devotion!" she sighs, calming. It certainly is what *Maman* would call *un spectacle*.

Unbound bosoms jiggle and sway, hips thrust forward and back, eyes are wide and staring, mouths mumble, drool, and call upon Father Divine. The God himself seems to take all this as his due, and calmly continues to wield his fork and knife.

My gaze keeps returning to Charmed Soul. I want to see how her devotion will possess her. I want to see her hair come loose from its stern braid and her slim torso dance. I want to see her feeling this passion. I want to see her control disturbed. But she alone among her sisters remains calm. Sad, defeated, she looks the very picture of a child left lonely on a playground where other, swifter children have abandoned her. Is her love of God not strong enough? The poor darling! As I am thinking this, she raises her head and our eyes meet.

Charmed Soul
Now that I have at last vibrated, I believe Father will hold me in higher esteem, but that does not happen. Perhaps He sees into my greedy, selfish heart. Perhaps He sees that some of the love that must be His I now hold for my pretty girl, and that images of her lodge themselves in my heart, affecting my corporeal form with sinful degradation. Father must see this in me, for He tells Many Acts of Love to say how I am no longer a Sweet and I am even removed from managing the banquet, though previously He had praised my efforts. I am now washing floors and lavatories in another heaven. "Work hard and hope there is no retribution!" Many Acts of Love scolds me. I am lucky, for the newest Sweet, Eternal Life, has drawn attention away from my disgrace, taking the seat at Father's right hand, the very closest. I have failed my God.

Mimi LaRouge
I have been to every one of Father Divine's banquet halls over the past month, and I cannot find her. No one I ask will help me. If I

could get close enough, I would go right up to that God's table and ask him what has been done with my Charmed Soul, but he is too well protected. I am worse than the worst of the girls who cry and run after joes they've convinced themselves are their only, their true sweethearts. But Charmed Soul has grown to fill my heart, every small part of it. I believe that she, too, was growing fond of me. I saw it in how she strode over to make sure my glass was filled with water, how she straightened the flowers on my table, offered me fresh pie, hot from the oven. And there was that time she passed by and brushed against the back of my chair and my coat fell. She gasped, then stooped to pick it up, smoothed it and shook it, blushing, holding it out to me. As I took it, our hands touched and fire kindled between us. She went to move away, but I held her fingers until she had to tug herself free. Oh, and where is she now?

Charmed Soul
I am very alone. God has withdrawn Himself from me. I fear retri-bution. After my chores at this new heaven, I walk and walk and walk. I wander Central Park, which, though tamed, is still more natural than sidewalks and buildings and paved streets. When I am almost dead with weariness, I allow myself to rest on the lawn, the poor, trodden-to-bits remnant of grass.

Mimi LaRouge
How strange that after haunting every heaven I could find, I prac-tically tumble over her here in Central Park. She is sitting on the grass, her feet tucked up beneath her. I join her. She raises her head and I see that perhaps she has been crying, but she greets me as they all do, "Peace."

"Peace," I say, then, "I've missed you at the banquet! Aren't you working there anymore?" I think I may have been too forward, as her expression darkens, but it is only that she is indeed very troubled. She tells me she is no longer a Sweet. "He fired you?" I am indignant. She smiles a little and shakes her head, and then the whole story comes out, how she must not have been fully giving of herself, how God must see into her heart where she is surely holding something back, how she has tried and tried but only keeps being assigned different and more unpleasant tasks, how she knows it's her own fault.

She touches my arm and says earnestly, "If only I could go back to our heaven in the country, perhaps there I could prove myself to Father!" It is quiet around us as we watch a squirrel scramble up the trunk of a tree. He shakes his tail and scolds down at us. "He is very vexed!" exclaims Charmed Soul, and I see how she loves nature and all things in nature. I feel for that moment that even if her God cannot, I see right down into her loving and generous heart.

Charmed Soul

I feel that I am floating, that this lawn here in poor old Central Park is a sturdy raft or a flying carpet and that Mimi—her name is Mimi! —calls me on to some great adventure down the Mississippi or into the scented air of Arabia. There are other people walking by, even sitting near us, but we possess a private scrap of the park for just us alone. She watches me and listens and is kind. It could be that I will regret it later, but on our raft of green, I tell Mimi my worries and as I do, my heart lightens. I do not tell her about my doubts, but I wonder what those friendly eyes read in my face. I almost feel that she can see my thoughts and that she knows what I am only now coming to understand myself: if I have failed my God, it is perhaps only because (oh, dare I even say it?) He has first failed me.

Mimi LaRouge

It is late. Charlie is late. I have bribed my roommate to go and sleep in another girl's room tonight, a common practice among us, and I'm sure she thinks some joe is on his way to me. But it is my Charlie who taps on the door at last, my Charlie who comes shyly but with much determination into my small room. I stand up to embrace her and she is stiff, so stiff. Does she know this is why I invited her? Did I misinterpret her sighs and glances as we spoke in Central Park? No, now she relaxes. Now she clings to me.

"I was jealous of your God," I murmur to her, thinking of that time when all the Sweets were filled with divine love. "I felt almost angry. *I* wanted that from you!"

She is trembling, and says nothing. Her heart beats against my chest, and I am suddenly heedless, desirous, and impatient.

"Won't you undress?" I say, pulling back and shucking out of my own clothes as quickly as I can. I want them off! It feels so good to be alfresco, as *Maman* always jokingly called it. Alfresco and on view for my Charlie.

"You are so beautiful!" she says, then shyly bows her head, but not before I see her eyes gleaming. She manages to remove her outer layer, but at her cotton undershirt and slip, she hesitates. She sits on the bed, and I sit close beside her.

I lean into her and reach out to take up the very end of her braid. I pull off the string she's tied it with, and slowly begin to separate the strands. When I'm finished, I place both hands on her cheeks and kiss her forehead between the wings of her hair. She blushes and stays very still. I move behind her on the bed, lean against the wall, and draw her close between my legs so her back rests against me. I spoon myself to her, the rough weave of her undershirt delicious on my nipples, the slick of her smooth slip lovely on my cleft. I do know to tread lightly with girls like my Charlie. I do know that. I press close, I rub my body on her. Oh, the darling! She can't hide it. She is breathing, sighing, and helping me to rub. She need not turn around, though, my skittish thoroughbred. For this first time, I will carry her and bring her along.

Charlie
My heart is swelling, all my limbs, my breast, my belly, oh, she slides on me, the clothing between us, conducting our heat. Leave me my clothing, Mimi! I beg without speaking, and she does, though she is gorgeous and naked, only slipping a hand onto my thigh, right to the edge of my drawers, then her fingers feel under the rim into the crease of my thigh. I make some strangled sound and she stops but starts again, creeping, creeping her fingers into the very soft middle of me, where no one has ever felt but I want her to feel it, it is the feel of bells ringing and shouting hallelujah and of being outside during a thunderstorm with lightning striking all around. She is against the wall and I am snug between her legs and I can feel her pressing against me, moving herself against my back, all the while creeping and pattering with her fingers. I grasp the coverlet in bunches, I close my eyes, I move my hips back toward her, then up against her darting fingers. I feel her breasts, heavy and full against my back; she wriggles, takes one of my hands and puts it between us and I try to creep my fingers around and into her as she is doing to me. My hair is all over my face, I am laughing, I am crying, we squirm like snakes entwined how damp she is there, a pool of golden, I know it is golden, as my fingers can feel color, can understand more than fingers ever have about creeping about pattering to and fro where fingers must find their purpose, a purpose hidden from me until today. Her fingers play their rhythm and her hips thrust and reach to mine and I press back, she presses front, oh fingers! oh moist and damp and warm and golden!

Mimi LaRouge

After our release, our climax, our *petite mort*, I move to the floor and kneel before her, bringing her face to mine so we can finally kiss. I find those thin, supple lips, her tongue swollen from her calls of pleasure.

We will leave New York, we will leave her God and the joes behind, we will return to the country where we both belong. We will live on my family's farm and *Maman* and Daddy will take my thoroughbred into their bosoms and we will escape retribution and we will live as we please and no one will harm us.

I shall teach her French, I shall walk with her in our woods. I will do whatever she needs and we will make our own heaven and prepare our own banquet and set a place for our deity there and sit down together and feast on love.

ABOUT THE AUTHORS

VALERIE ALEXANDER (valeriealexander.org) lives in LA. Her stories have been published in a number of anthologies and sci-fi and speculative magazines.

M. BIRDS (mbirds.ca) is a mad queer writer and musician from Vancouver, British Columbia. Her short fiction has previously been published by Freaky Fountain Press, Cleis Press, and Hot Ink Press.

NAT BURNS (natburns.org) is an award-winning author and journalist and is a book editor for several publishers. She has published fifteen novels to date and her shorter work has appeared in more than thirty anthologies. Her music review column, "Notes from Nat," appears monthly in *Lesbian News Magazine*.

EMILY L. BYRNE's (writeremilylbyrne.blogspot.com) stories have appeared in *Forbidden Fruit*; *Best Lesbian Erotica: 20th Anniversary Edition*; *Best Lesbian Erotica of the Year, Vol. 2*; *Witches,*

Princesses and Women at Arms; and *Blood in the Rain 3.* She is the author of *Knife's Edge: Kinky Lesbian Erotica* and *Desire: Sensual Lesbian Erotica.*

LEA DALEY (leadaley.com) has written fiction while raising children, claiming a lesbian identity, earning a BFA, and directing a United Way childcare center. Her debut novel, *Waiting for Harper Lee,* was a Golden Crown Awards finalist. Her second book, *FutureDyke,* won a 2015 Goldie Award and was a Lambda Literary finalist.

NANISI BARRETT D'ARNUK has traveled around the world to gather information for her writing. She has five novels, several novellas, and many short stories published, ranging from mysteries to sweet or erotic romances. More are in process. A new-age political thriller will be published this fall.

R. G. EMANUELLE (dirtroadbooks.com) is a writer and editor living in New York City. She is the author of novels, novellas, and short stories, as well as coeditor of several anthologies, including the Lambda Literary finalist *All You Can Eat.* She is a cofounder and coowner of Dirt Road Books.

MAGS HAYWARD writes MF and FF erotic romance. Her debut novella, *The Devil on Her Shoulder,* was published in January 2017. She is currently working on a full-length novel and additional short erotica. Originally from North Wales, Mags lives in Worcestershire, United Kingdom.

VICTORIA JANSSEN's (victoriajanssen.com) *The Duke and the Pirate Queen* (2010) is set in the same universe as her first novel, *The Duchess, Her Maid, The Groom, and Their Lover* (2008).

SOMMER MARSDEN has been called " . . . one of the top storytellers in the erotica genre" (Violet Blue) and "Unapologetic" (Alison Tyler). Her erotic novels include *Restless Spirit* and *Learning to Drown*. Professional dirty word writer, gluten-free baker, amateur runner, vintage addict, old wiener-dog walker, and expert procrastinator.

T. C. MILL (TC-Mill.com) writes and runs an editing business in the Midwest, one answer to the question "What do you *do* with a philosophy degree?" Her stories have appeared in the *Mofo Pubs Presents* anthologies, on the websites *Nerve* and *Bright Desire*, and in *Best Women's Erotica of the Year, Vol. 2.*

R. D. MILLER is currently based in Halifax, Canada. She spent most of her adult life living "away" and is getting reacquainted with Nova Scotia by visiting all the craft breweries. She has always loved storytelling and will talk your ear off over a beer or two if you let her.

SCOUT RHODES is a middle-aged butch farmer who lives in western Massachusetts. She is a writer, an illustrator, and a book designer. Her butch paramour lives in San Francisco.

PASCAL SCOTT's short fiction has appeared in *Thunder of War, Lightning of Desire: Lesbian Historical Military Erotica*; *Through the Hourglass: Lesbian Historical Romance; Order Up: A Menu of Lesbian Romance and Erotica; Unspeakably Erotic: Lesbian Kink;* and *Best Lesbian Erotica, Vol. 2 (2017)*. She lives in Decatur, GA.

RAVEN SKY is a polyamorous queer femme from Canada. Although she has published frequently, this is her first erotic publication. She is pleased to be interesting enough to merit a *nom de plume*. She is displeased to be in a profession straitlaced enough to necessitate it.

ANNA WATSON, perhaps because she grew up in a stone-cold atheist household, has always been fascinated by the lengths people will go to for God. Father Divine was extremely forward thinking in terms of race, and did indeed provide meals to all comers during the Depression; the rest is all Anna's toothsome imagination.

XAN WEST (xanwest.wordpress.com) has been published in over thirty-five erotica anthologies. Xan's "First Time Since" won honorable mention for the 2008 NLA John Preston Short Fiction Award. Xan's collection *Show Yourself to Me* was described by M. Christian as "a book that changes what erotica can and should be."

SACCHI GREEN (sacchi-green.blogspot.com, facebook.com/ sacchi.green) is a Lambda Award–winning editor and writer who lives in the five-college area of western Massachusetts, retreats to the mountains of New Hampshire whenever possible, and makes occasional forays into the real world. Her work appears in scores of books, including nine editions of *Best Lesbian Erotica*, and she's edited fifteen anthologies, including *Best Lesbian Erotica of the Year: 20th Anniversary Edition*; *Best Lesbian Erotica of the Year, Vol. 2*; and *Witches, Princesses and Women at Arms: Erotic Lesbian Fairy Tales*.